HUNTING THE *DRAGON*

A NOVEL

HUNTING
THE *DRAGON*

A NOVEL

PETER DIXON

HYPERION
NEW YORK

Printed in the United States of America

First Edition

1   3   5   7   9   10   8   6   4   2

V567-9638-5-10015

Library of Congress Cataloging-in-Publication Data on file.
ISBN 978-1-4231-2498-6

This book is set in 12-point Adobe Garamond Pro.
Reinforced binding

Visit WWW.HYPERIONBOOKSFORCHILDREN.COM

THIS LABEL APPLIES TO TEXT STOCK

To Marilyn and Paul Stader
for friendship and helping hands

ACKNOWLEDGMENTS

First, the dolphins. Thank you all for swimming among us, for inspiring compassion and bringing joy. We're better humans because you exist in the wild. Your deaths in the nets have fostered empathy for your kind in most of us.

Thanks to all ocean defenders and warriors who fight the constant battle against the needless slaughter of dolphins and whales, and even sharks. Thanks to all who give their time and effort to protect the sea from the ever-growing waste flushed down rivers from our factories and cities, dumped from garbage scows and ships into the oceans. Then there's the disposable military ordnance, chemical and nuclear, carelessly consigned to the depths. Thanks to the Cousteau family for taking us underwater and opening our eyes to the beauty of *The Silent World*. I'm indebted to Paul Watson of Sea Shepherd, the Greenpeace activists, and Sam LeBuddie, whose video brought about international awareness of the killing of dolphins to catch tuna. Good fortune to all who are fighting to stop the slaughter of whales and dolphins and the ever-rising tide of human assault on the seas.

I'm grateful to my longtime friend, the late pioneer marine biologist Dr. Rimmon C. Fay, who saw the future decades ago and inspired me by his wisdom to help protect the ocean's fragile health. Included among those who care is Hugo Verlomme, a fellow waterman, who first read the manuscript, found merit in my work, and took the risk of publishing this book in France. David Konig's skill in translating English to French gave the manuscript art and life. Thank you both. When help was needed most, Chris Palmer, wildlife film producer and founder of the Center for Environmental Filmmaking, offered generous support.

Editorial assistance and enthusiasm far beyond the norm was graciously given by my super agent Albert Zuckerman of Writers House, and editor Wendy Lefkon of Hyperion Books. Pahl Dixon's careful review and typo-hunting skills helped the manuscript find its way into readers' hands.

So many people have helped to me live by, on, and, briefly, under the sea. I thank you all. Most of all, I shout out my deep love for Sarah Dixon, who swims by my side through life—loving, caring, and laughing.

INTRODUCTION

Many people—good friends, colleagues, and those I've met on my life's journey—contributed to the writing of this novel. The chilling story that Phil Eastley told me of his experiences on a tuna clipper was the motivating moment that set me on the path to write this book. Phil was perhaps the first to dive into a purse seine to save netted dolphins—and he was made to suffer for his compassion.

Dolphins—bless them for their exuberance and joyousness. I first swam with dolphins at the old Marineland sea park in Palos Verdes, California, under the watchful eye of Dr. David Brown, curator of marine mammals. David helped me to understand their physiology and spiritual side. I'm also indebted to my mentor, film director Paul Stader and his wife, Marilyn, who believed that this young diver could be depended on underwater. Paul invited me to join the stunt divers on the old *Sea Hunt* TV series. That path led to meeting producer Ivan Tors, who was launching a series about a dolphin named Flipper.

While Ivan was waiting for NBC to decide to broadcast *Flipper* I decided to write an episode on my own. The moment I heard that the network had bought *Flipper* I presented the script to Ivan. Then I waited. Ivan called next week. He remarked, "This one's too long. I'll shoot it as a two-parter. And I want you to write the first episode." I went on to write many more scripts about that remarkable dolphin and her human family. Yes, *her*. Flipper was in reality female.

Work for the Cousteau Society brought me into contact with dolphins again. Writing books and filming documentaries with my wife, Sarah, in Japan, Mexico, Trinidad, El Salvador, Canada, New Zealand, and many other coastal countries also allowed swims with dolphins. Then came Phil Eastley's moving account of dolphins' slaughter in the nets for dollar-a-can tuna . . . and this book was born some years later. Thank you, Phil.

In closing, I must state that all the characters in this novel are fictitious and any resemblance to persons living or dead is coincidental.

Peter Dixon
Malibu, California

CHAPTER ONE

He stood in the open boat and looked far out to sea. The afternoon glare burned his eyes, but he could see that the huge swells breaking over Bombora Reef, Fiji, were still possible to surf. His stomach muscles tightened and he noticed his heart was pounding. He wondered if his tension was from excitement or fear.

As Billy watched the swells break and become surfing waves, he peeled a flake of sunburned skin off his tender nose. He flicked it away, and the tiny fragment of dried human bark landed on the water beside the skiff. He wondered how many layers of skin he had left to offer the sea. It was time to slather another coat of sunblock on his nose. Distracted by the surf boiling over the reef, he forgot. Then he saw a small fish dart from the coral and his flake of nose tissue went down its mouth.

Except where his body was covered by faded heavy-duty red nylon surfing trunks, Billy glowed a healthy brown. But no amount of sunscreen created a strong enough barrier against the bombardment of ultraviolet rays that daily tanned his muscular eighteen-year-old surfer's body. His whole torso was a case of skin cancer waiting to happen. He didn't care. Since Billy Crawford had been an airhead Southern Californian sun-bronzed ten-year-old, the surfing addiction had grabbed him with a force stronger than food, girls, or money.

He was in Fiji fulfilling his dream of a surfer's endless summer by working his way around the oceans of the world. His search for the perfect wave was a consuming goal and the reason he had decided to skip college for a couple of years.

Bombora Island was the primo place to find the ultimate wave. Better yet, he had a job as a surf-taxi wrangler, running boatloads of guests from the Bombora Surf Camp out to Bombora Reef, four miles offshore. At the reef he would anchor the skiff in deep water off to the side of the break. There he'd lifeguard the surfers until they were so exhausted they could barely paddle toward another wave.

He stared at the giant, storm-born swells rolling in from the Tasman Sea far to the south and sensed they were growing even larger. The swells, which would soon become perfect surf, marched in relentlessly. For an instant before they broke, the crests hovered as if not wanting to end their long journey. Then the swells destroyed themselves in white-maned explosions on this remote Fijian coral reef.

At Bombora Reef, the gigantic waves formed a shoulder: part churning crest, part smooth unbroken slope. On a curling

Bombora wave a skilled surfer could ride a half mile and more. These were the waves that the guests he was responsible for had traveled halfway around the world to challenge.

Billy leaned against the warm shroud of a Yamaha 50-horsepower outboard motor and judged that they were breaking an honest sixteen feet from crest to trough. *Best surf in three months, and getting bigger.*

He had anchored the boat where the reef descended into a deepwater channel. It was so deep, he believed, that no wave could possibly break here. Not far beyond the launch, and just in front of the churning white water, was the only spot where a surfer could take off safely. To be caught inside a wave's crushing maw meant a horrendous wipeout, followed by a pounding on the sharp coral that lay waiting only feet below the surface.

He watched enviously as the surfers he had taxied out to Bombora Reef paddled frantically to position themselves for these dangerous but nearly perfect waves. One of them turned, took three strokes, and began sliding down the steep face of a tunneling breaker. He stood, and a second later, white water cascaded around him. The surfer angled steeply downward gaining speed. Near the bottom he turned and accelerated across the translucent moving wall of water and raced ahead of the curling shoulder. Then he slowed, allowing the wave to tunnel over him. Billy saw him vanish inside the tube and feared he would be pounded onto the reef. As the wave collapsed, tons of falling water compressed the air inside the rolling cylinder. The air then exploded out of the open end of the tunnel, shooting the surfer safely out of the wave.

Billy was stoked by the surfer's fantastic ride and thrust

his fists into the air in self-congratulation.

What am I doing in the boat? Billy asked himself. He grabbed his nine-foot big wave board and leaped over the side. Three minutes later he paddled into the lineup with the other surfers.

A huge swell passed under Billy's surfboard and he was lifted skyward. He looked out to sea and gasped. "Oh, no! Here they come!" What he saw was a series of giant, jagged-edged moving mountains rushing toward them. He knew these swells would produce waves of such size and force, such violence and speed, that very few surfers could survive a wipeout if they were fool enough to ride one. They were true killer waves—one of nature's most powerful phenomena.

Alone, he would have gone for it, because he knew Bombora Reef and the exact moment to launch down the wave's slope. Today was different, and Billy hesitated. The massive swells charging toward them would totally dominate the surfers he had been hired to protect. Billy stuck two fingers in his mouth and whistled a loud blast. His shrill warning carried across the open water to the seven wave riders sitting dumbly astride their boards, unaware of the coming watery avalanche.

Seven heads turned as one to stare at Billy and saw him pointing frantically at the horizon. He screamed the one word they would all understand and respond to: *"Outside!"*

They heard Billy and knew that something dangerous was approaching.

The surfers saw the awesome swells and began paddling rapidly seaward in a desperate attempt to escape before it was too late.

Billy stroked furiously, making sure the surfers were all moving out to sea. He studied the swells and knew there was a good chance one might break in the channel where the launch was anchored. It was all happening too fast. He thought fearfully, Without the boat, we've had it.

They all made it over the first of the giant crests. He looked seaward. More mountainous swells marched toward them. They gotta be twenty-five feet!, he thought as he paddled up the face of the next one. He made it over the top, as did the rest of the surfers. The outside swells were even larger.

There were four more in the set, all killers, all so pregnant with force that anyone caught in the impact zone would be battered and held down longer than a panting, exhausted surfer could survive. And then there was a real danger of being jammed between the coral heads.

He glanced at the boat as a house-high swell passed under the hull. The bow lifted and the anchor line grew dangerously taut. Would it hold? Would a wave swamp their only link to the surf camp? There wasn't time to worry about his dumb decision to surf instead of stay on the boat. He had to get his flock of frightened, gasping surfers to safety.

"Paddle! Damn it! Paddle!" he bellowed, feeling his shoulder muscles ache from the tremendous strain. Two of the stronger, more experienced surfers were angling for the channel, knowing that deeper water would retard the swells from breaking. The others took their lead and followed. An overweight, out-of-shape kid began to fall behind. He turned to Billy. Between fearful gasps he yelled, "I'm not going to make it!"

All Billy could do was scream, "Paddle!"

A monster swell rushed down on them, looming so tall it cast a dark, ominous shadow. The thundering roar, and the hiss of moisture-laden air displaced by the towering bulk of the wave, combined to send a stab of fear deep into Billy's guts.

He took another few deep strokes and reached the winded kid. The surfer's eyes were wide with dread and his arms dug in feebly. Billy knew he was spent. He had two choices—help the guy, or leave him. If the exhausted surfer went over the falls and was caught in the maelstrom of breaking waves and jagged coral, he would die. Billy did the only thing he could: try to save him. As the swell began to break, he shoved the surfer's board up the swell's face with all the strength he had left.

As he pushed the kid upward, he lost his own momentum. His board began sliding backward down the wave's steep front. He would be blasted and buried if he didn't make a desperate move for survival. With a last look at the surfer, who was scrambling over the top of the breaking crest, Billy flipped his board around and took one deep stroke down the wave's near-vertical face.

His takeoff was impossibly late, but the wave seemed to hesitate an instant before it slammed down. The reprieve gave Billy a microsecond to come to his feet and push the nose of his board downward. The cresting wave was so steep he almost pitchpoled, but his stance was perfect and he retained control. As he shot toward the trough, he shifted his inside foot back and pressed downward. The board's fin dug in and he began the critical bottom turn. Deep in the dark wet valley of the wave, he trimmed the board and raced from the monster that was plunging down on him. His speed was now so great that it carried him ahead of the collapsing wave and out onto its shoulder. Billy was going so fast that his board hummed with the fin's vibration. He could have ridden on to the channel, where the wave's great force would dissipate in deeper water, but there was the boat and the other surfers. He angled upward, flew over the top of the wave and out of its grip.

Billy dropped over the backside and saw a huge rogue swell rolling down on the anchored boat. He prayed that it wouldn't break on the frail fiberglass hull. His prayer wasn't granted. Ten yards in front of the boat the giant wave crashed down. The launch, outboard, seats, and life preservers were blasted free. It was as if Neptune's trident had smashed their means of survival into atoms.

Well outside the waves' impact zone, Billy gathered the panicked surfers together. As they caught their breath and fought down fear, Billy glanced at the sun. Three hours of daylight left. They could attempt paddling back to the surf camp, but he knew that the fast-moving current was against them. In the darkness they'd likely miss the island. If they failed to reach Bombora, the next landfall was Tonga, six hundred miles to the southeast. Or they could wait here until someone missed them and dispatched another boat. Then Billy remembered he wasn't expected back until dark. If rescue didn't come before nightfall, they might not be found at all. He could just see the island through the mist created by the huge surf pounding the reef.

He stared at the shaken, gasping surfers. They were beginning to shiver. Was it from the breeze chilling their wet, exhausted bodies, or from shock? Their lives were in his hands, and he thought, It's time to play leader and show some confidence.

With forced calm, he told them, "We're paddling back. So, pair up and stick together. We'll be easier to spot in a group."

"I'll never make it," said the chubby surfer Billy had saved.

Another glared at Billy and muttered, "You should have stayed in the boat."

"Yeah, tell me about it," he answered trying to sound tough. "Let's go, unless you want to hang around here for the reef sharks. They feed at night."

They had paddled two of the four miles when the sun touched the horizon. The current was flowing against them and they were making slow progress. Billy took a bearing on an early rising star and judged the direction of the wind and current. If he missed the camp in the darkness, they were dead. He tried to jolly his increasingly fearful group, "Hey, we're doing great. I bet they'll save supper for us. Come on, only a couple miles more."

In the fading light, the silhouette of Bombora Island, low in the sea and etched with the jagged fringes of coco palms, vanished in the growing dimness. He called a break and promised that salvation was only a short paddle away. "We can do it, guys. An hour more!"

Twelve minutes later darkness came with an abrupt, tropic suddenness. Billy heard one of the surfers whisper, "Dear God, don't let me die out here."

He shouted at him to knock it off, and said it was their guts that would save their lives. He felt the same fear, but added,

"They'll be out looking for us. It'll just be a few minutes. Hang in there and keep paddling."

There was no moon and Billy was beginning to doubt they'd make the island. On his exhausted shoulders hung the knowledge that he was responsible for this disaster.

Something long and dark whooshed past his surfboard and he instinctively pulled his arms out of the water. Was it a white-tipped reef shark, a green venomous sea snake, or what? One of the others cried out, "Sharks!"

"Shut up and keep paddling," Billy threatened.

Another black form appeared and slowed beside Billy. He heard a of rush of air and felt warm moisture drift down on him. Then came a burst of rapid click-ticks, followed by a high-pitched whistling. He peered into the darkness and drew back as a rounded beak emerged from the water next to his leg. Behind the snout was a bulbous head and Billy cried out, "Hey, guys. We lucked out. They're dolphins! We don't have to worry about sharks now."

The shadowy cetaceans took up positions forward of the group. Billy imagined they were pointing the way back to the island and told the surfers to follow them. They paddled another five minutes, refreshed by their convoy of spouting escorts. Suddenly, the dolphins vanished. He sensed their disappearance was for a reason. He called for a rest, and told everyone to be silent. Three minutes passed. His dread came boiling up again. Then he heard the familiar sound of an idling Yamaha outboard. Billy whistled louder than he had ever whistled before. A handheld searchlight probed through the darkness. Then a voice boomed across the water, "Hey, Billy! We're coming!"

He recognized Druku's deep baritone and thanked the Fijian gods of old for placing this good-natured, smiling personification of the bula spirit of hospitality aboard the rescue boat. Nobody but Druku could have found them in the darkness.

"What are you doing paddling back, Billy?" Druku asked as he helped him aboard the launch.

"You know me. I went surfin' when I should have stayed in the boat. The waves took it."

"Figures, bro."

"How'd you find us in the dark?"

"The dolphins . . ."

Billy offered a silent prayer of thanks and asked, "Do you think they really led you to us?"

"No doubt about it, Billy. They're sea children, like us."

In the surf camp's palm-thatched lodge, the surfers who Billy had saved were drinking beer and were bragging about the biggest bitchin' waves ever, and telling stories about the giant surf that almost drowned them. Billy sat off to the side with the young, out-of-shape surfer, who still had that haunted look of fear in his eyes. He smiled ruefully at Billy and said, "You know, nobody ever did anything like what you did for me. I wouldn't have made it without you, Billy."

He gave the surfer a modest grin. "I guess we'll both remember today for a long, long time."

Later, after the exhausted surfers stumbled into the night, the owner of the surfing camp took Billy aside and said in a low, regretful voice, "You screwed up, Billy. If Druku hadn't found you . . ."

"I'll stay in the boat from now on, okay?"

"What boat? You knew not to surf with the guests when you were the only guide on the reef. You broke that rule and almost drowned those guys. You're a good boatman, Billy, but I can't take another chance on you. You're fired."

"Hey, but I got 'em back—"

"You're out of here on Tuesday's boat to Suva."

CHAPTER TWO

The aging leader of the pod pointed his grayish, bone-hard beak eastward, guiding the dolphins for the west coast of Central America. The old dolphin was incredibly swift and strong, even after thirty-seven seasons of migrating across the Pacific. He and his pod of two hundred and seventy-three spinners were shepherding a hundred and fifty times their number of yellowfin tuna. When he had first made the cross-ocean journey at his mother's side, the pod had been larger, much larger; but that was before the nets.

The dolphins were swimming fast, navigating by instinct, toward the eastern tropical Pacific off the shore of Central America. Near the coast they would find massed schools of anchovies and other small fish that the dolphins and the tuna would feed on. Though the dolphins had a dependable source of rich, oily protein close at hand.

The old spinner was flanked by his captains and sergeants—younger males waiting their turn to lead—followed by uncles and cousins who patrolled the flanks and brought up the rear of the vast, fast-moving, leaping and diving throng. It was this alliance between dolphins and tuna—this evolutionary partnership—that was rapidly bringing about the extinction of the dolphins.

Out here, in the vast open ocean between Fiji and the Americas, where the sleek, air-breathing dolphins surged eastward, little life quivered or swam. So, the old spinner, his hungry pod, and the tuna they accompanied, hurried for their ancestral feeding grounds—and the mile-long red nylon nets of the fishermen anticipating their arrival.

Yellowfin tuna and their dolphin escorts migrated across the central Pacific long before prehumans wandered the plains of East Africa's Serengeti, and even before the mastodons of the Ice Age lay down to freeze on Canadian tundra. The spinners, and sometimes spotted and common dolphins, evolved a symbiotic life-and-death partnership with the yellowfin, and each species depends on the other to survive. It is a simple arrangement involving food.

Dolphins and tuna are highly efficient carnivores. They subsist on smaller, schooling fish that usually swim in tight-knit groups for survival. Tuna feed off the trailing edge of these dense balls of small fish, and the laggards who leave the group. Not enough of the small-fry abandon the biomass to satisfy the hunger of these huge schools—of three, to five, and even ten thousand yellowfin.

Enter the exuberant dolphins, who seem to take great

joy in ramming their bony beaks through the balled bait fish, exploding the dense pack, and crushing them into swallowable size with their powerful toothed jaws. Then the tuna feast on the scattered, terrorized school. Over the millennia both species have cooperated in the hunt to ease their ravenous hunger, and their migrations continue today.

Dolphins, with their smiling faces, are boisterous, joyous animals. They suckle their young, surface to breathe, then spout their watery vapor skyward. Often they leap from the sea, sometimes very high, sometimes twisting, then plunge back to glide underwater until the want of air drives them into the sunlight once again.

Mothers teach their young with firm loving nudges of their beaks. Fathers sense predatory sharks rocketing for the pups and elderly, and charge to drive them off. Courtship continues day and night with touching and poking, and sometimes bites. Gangs of curious juveniles coming of age race each other, butting and ramming, testing their prowess. Their journey of life is a marvel only surpassed by the question of how the stars found their places in the heavens.

The old leader, his echolocating clicks ranging far forward of the pod, picked up a signal bounced off a small school of bait fish. That was unusual here in the open sea of the central Pacific. His biological sonar pinged louder and detected other shapes. Food was ahead, but there was something else. He swam faster and echolocated again.

Two images entered the fantastic neural array of his melonlike forehead. They were floating on the surface of the water and had air spaces inside their body cavities like his kind. There was another form, inert and wooden, bigger than the biggest blue whale, that lay motionless beside the two unknown living forms. The lifeless, drifting bulk didn't concern the leader. There was no fearful, entangling mesh webbing spilling off the stern to trap them.

Closer now, he sent out another burst of energy from his brain's transponder. The returns from his pinging now gave the old spinner a detailed impression. They were mammals like himself, with lungs, stomachs, and bony skeletons. He sensed no danger and felt only a curiosity to know more. With a strong beat of his wide fluke, the old spinner charged ahead, homing on the fish and the unfamiliar mammalian figures beside the long whalelike object that drifted on the calm surface of the central Pacific.

Floating on the warm undulating sea, the young woman could see nothing but long streaks of wavering blue that angled downward into the abyss. She peered through the cyclops eye of her diver's mask and watched the blueness change to gray, then fade to darkness where no light penetrated.

The fact that the bottom was twenty-three thousand feet below was decidedly unsettling. Sarah imagined she was sinking, like the ballpoint pen she had accidentally dropped overboard yesterday. The image of the pen descending down, down, down into nothingness unnerved her.

Her companion suddenly lowered his broad, muscular shoulders, bent at the waist, and dove. With powerful beats of his swim fins he kicked downward. She watched him descend rapidly into the dimness, so deep that she feared he might vanish altogether. Sarah guessed he reached seventy feet before he stopped to hover, but the underwater visibility was so fantastic she couldn't really judge his depth. She realized there was no need to fear for Benny. He was in his element, at one with the sea. She admired this burly man. No, she told herself, it was more than admiration. Benny Seeger had been her girlhood hero, her activist icon. His commitment to saving whales and dolphins, his deeds of moral and physical courage, had drawn her to him. Sarah wondered if she might be infatuated with Benny. She told herself that that was crazy. She was only eighteen. Then she wondered what it would be like to fall in love with a man certainly old enough to be her father. She knew that the other young women who had volunteered to sail aboard *Salvador* were mad for him. Why shouldn't I find him attractive? she thought.

He turned and kicked slowly for the surface, lazily twisting and turning as if simulating a giant, barrel-shaped grouper. She was envious of Benny and his relaxed togetherness with the sea. He was a water person. She was not. Being afloat on all that profound vastness made her decidedly uncomfortable.

Benny glanced upward, not wanting to smack into the barnacle-encrusted bottom of the old *Salvador*. He made a mental note to have her wooden hull scraped when they docked in Fiji to refit and refuel. In the hunt to come he would need every knot of speed the surplus ex–Canadian Navy minesweeper could produce from her well-worn engines.

As his need for air grew stronger he kicked harder. His gaze shifted from the ship's hull to Sarah's pleasing, backlit outline.

He liked what he saw, and the way her long blond hair caught the light as it waved in the gentle swells.

Better yet, Benny thought, she was smart and dedicated. And she and her father had worked like hell to raise all that money for this crazy voyage.

Now desperate for oxygen, he surfaced beside Sarah, spit out his snorkel, and sucked in air. With a grin he said happily, "God, I love it out here!"

She didn't share his good feeling about the ocean and replied, "It's so hypnotic, it seems to draw you to the bottom."

"Yeah, right. But I love it! I wish I could hold my breath for an hour."

"You would."

"Say again," he asked, turning his good ear toward her.

"It's nothing," Sarah answered, remembering he had blown his left eardrum twice by diving too deep. She wondered why he didn't give it up.

During the long weeks of their voyage, Sarah and Captain Seeger had developed a close big brother–little sister friendship. They were at ease with each other, and despite his responsibility of command, Benny never put up emotional barriers between himself and his crew. They loved and respected their captain. When Benny gave an order, the twenty-three young men and women who had joined him on his quest responded willingly.

Suddenly, the old dolphin's burst of echolocating, click-ticking energy sounded in their ears. Then the pod all echolocated at once on the two swimmers treading water beside the wood-hulled ship. The massed concentration of sound physically bombarded their bodies and the man and young woman peered underwater seeking the source.

Sarah saw nothing and spun to grab Benny. "What's that?" she demanded.

"What we've been busting our butts looking for. Stay cool. They'll be here any minute."

As the pinging grew more intense, Sarah panicked and sprinted for *Salvador*. She reached the slippery wooden step of the diver's ladder and hung on. Keeping her mask underwater, Sarah watched the ship's captain floating serenely off the stern.

Benny let out half a breath and slowly sank beneath the surface to meet them. He hovered twenty feet down and noticed that his usually loose body had become tense. They were coming, and though there was no physical danger, their swift appearance always startled him.

Click, tick, squeak, click, ping—the dolphins were racing closer. The energy of their sonar beat on Benny and he thought, Can you read the inscription on my class ring, or the scars on my head, or that damn plantar wart on the sole of my foot? I bet you can, my beauties. Come on, guys, where are you . . . ?

Seconds later he saw the faint shape of the old leader. Other gray forms with white-dotted flanks appeared in his tunneled underwater vision. They charged for him like living torpedoes. Astonished by their boldness, Benny flinched and drew back.

Only the old leader and three of the larger males paused to stare at the human floating before them. The others went after the bait fish gathered under *Salvador*'s 112-foot wooden hull. Seconds later the small school was no more. Only bits of scale and drifting offal remained, already sinking slowly downward to contribute to the seafloor's ooze. Then the old dolphin turned away and raced on with his pod, and Benny rocked in the swirling vortex of their passing.

He watched the dolphins vanish to the east and imagined traveling with them. He would take the lead and guide them past the huge nets set to entrap the tuna—and usually the dolphins that accompanied them. Benny knew he was fantasizing. He vowed that this time he would use his considerable skills and all the limited power under his command to stop the killing of these majestic creatures for the sake of dollar-a-can tuna.

Benny surfaced and swam for the ship, thinking, Yeah, this time, my beauties, I'm going to sink one of those pirate tuna clippers.

CHAPTER THREE

The rusting 268-foot tuna clipper *Lucky Dragon* eased her black steel hull against a Suva, Fiji, wharf. Deckhands tossed mooring lines to waiting dockworkers who gaped at the weathered ship, appreciating her sleek nautical design. She was modern, though sea-scoured, and only seven years out of San Diego's Campbell Shipyards. The clipper was originally named *Stella Maria* and had once belonged to the Valeria Brothers. Restrictive legislation, designed to reduce the killing of dolphins in tuna nets, hurt profits and the Valeria family sold the ship to a Mexican syndicate. Fishermen across the border were not bound by the United State's Marine Mammal Protection Act. They could kill any and all dolphins trapped in their nets without observers looking on, or having to pay stiff fines to the U.S. government for violations.

The Mexican businessmen who bought the *Stella Maria*

hired a captain with uncertain navigational skills. On his first voyage the skipper misread a SAT/NAV plot and put the tuna boat on the rocks off Clipperton Island. The pride of the Valeria Brothers appeared a total loss. The syndicate sold the hulk to the clipper's first mate—Louis Gandara, formally of colonial Portuguese Mozambique, Southern Africa—for a half million dollars. Gandara really knew electronic navigation. He had secretly reprogrammed the SAT/NAV computer to strand the *Stella Maria* on the reef without damaging her keel.

For another eight hundred thousand dollars spent on salvage tugs and repairs, Gandara, an ex–Portuguese Navy lieutenant and patrol boat commander, became owner/captain of a seventeen-million-dollar vessel. How he actually acquired the money to finance his dream remains a mystery to this day. Rumors coming out of Mozambique hinted that Gandara and his gunboat crew had robbed the Bank of Lourenco Marques, fled Portuguese East Africa, and vanished into the Indian Ocean.

All these events, the rumors say, had occurred on the eventful day that FRELIMO revolutionary troops entered Mozambique's capital to end Portugal's 475-year colonial rule. Neither Gandara, the crew, nor the gunboat, were ever seen again in African waters.

Locked in Captain Gandara's spacious cabin were the clipper's forged registration certificates declaring *Lucky Dragon's* nationality of convenience to be Panamanian, Costa Rican, or Liberian. Louis Gandara would present them to suspicious customs officials, port captains, and government agents demanding ship's papers. Also secured in the cabin were flags of the various nations that *Lucky Dragon* flew when Gandara needed to change the ship's identity.

The rest of the clipper was the same hodgepodge of international convenience and humanity—a German MAN diesel of 4,750 horsepower; Japanese Furuno radar; Dutch pilot radios; a Hughes 300 helicopter from Culver City, California; British Lister generators and air compressors; waxed mahogany paneling from Honduras lining the walls of Gandara's quarters; crockery from China; and ten Belgian FM .308 NATO automatic assault rifles with 5,000 rounds of ammunition filling the arms cabinet.

The first mate was Brazilian, the chief engineer Australian, an ex-army pilot from Fort Dodge, Iowa, flew the spotting helicopter, and the remainder of the thirty-seven crewmen were from various third-world ports they could never return to without fear of arrest. In the ship's hold, frozen solid amid tons of board-stiff tuna, lay the shark-mangled remains of a Fijian boatman.

Gandara peered down from the wide bridge, checking that the dock lines were secure. All was in order and he spoke to his first mate. "Mr. Santos, take a detail below and chip that man out of the ice."

"Às suas ordens," the mate replied in his native Brazilian Portuguese, so slurred from growing up in a Rio slum that Gandara winced. His own Portuguese had the cultivated accent of a Lisbon aristocrat.

The captain picked up the bridge phone and ordered the engine stopped. He spoke fluent English, laced with a slight Zulu accent that was a reflection of his African birth and the influence of his nanny. English was the language of convenience

24

aboard *Lucky Dragon* because Gandara usually sold his catch to multinational tuna packers managed or owned by Americans, and accepted payment only in U.S. dollars, euros, or gold.

Gandara scanned the docks and saw nothing unusual except a hearse waiting to take away the body for burial in the man's homeland. He relaxed and let the tension drain from his wide shoulders. He remembered he was short one boatman and called down to Santos, who was on the main deck assembling a detail to remove the hatch covering the refrigerated fish hold. "Mr. Santos, let the third mate handle that. I want you to find a replacement for that Fijian . . . someone who can work the seine skiff without falling overboard."

The captain believed that men obey for two reasons: fear and respect for their leaders. He used both to ensure his orders were carried out swiftly and without question. He needed Santos's loyalty and brutality to rule the crew. With the mate as an extension of his will, he could distance himself from the uneducated men he both detested and relied on.

Billy sat on the Suva Harbor seawall sketching a small, 32-foot-long Westsail sloop. For Billy, Suva Harbor, where the Bombora Surf Camp launch had left him a week ago, was a jumping-off spot to other islands where waves broke big and clean over remote tropic reefs.

Since he had first spotted the Westsail, he was drawn to portray her in bold, bright watercolors. The sloop's seaworthy hull, simple rigging, and cozy cabin cried out adventure. Knowing that the boat was for sale, and he couldn't buy her, was maddening.

Billy had a bigger problem. The price of passage to the out islands was more than what remained in his wallet. All the cash he had left, after a week in a boardinghouse plus meals, was 255 Fijian, about 140 U.S. dollars, enough to survive another week—if he gave up lunch. For the past five days Billy had been prowling the docks looking for work as a deckhand on an interisland freighter bound anywhere there might be waves. He had no other resources. He had no mother and father in the States to wire him money for a ticket home. His parents had split some years back, and then when he was ten his father died. A good-hearted aunt took him in when his mother remarried and moved away with her new husband. He wasn't sure where to find Mom now. His aunt had helped him so much over the years, his pride wouldn't allow him to ask for more.

Right now, on the Suva dock, Billy was as much an orphan as the sick little sea lion pups that sometimes washed up in front of his Venice Beach, Southern California, lifeguard tower. In his memory he could still see a gang of vicious beach kids poking sticks at one of the emaciated creatures. When they refused to stop tormenting the pup his anger overcame his better judgment and he hurled the whole group into the surf. A parent had complained to the chief lifeguard and Billy almost lost his first real job.

Billy's attention returned to his brush and watercolor pad. He wondered if he should add the FOR SALE sign in the cabin window. He had met the sloop's owner and his pregnant wife. She wanted to fly home and have the baby in a hospital. He was for sailing on, delivering the child himself. She won, and her mom had sent the money for the couple to return to the

States. Like Billy, they were broke, and the stubby little sailboat of their dreams, and his, would someday find a new owner.

He dabbed the tip of his brush in a water jar and worked on. Billy liked the way the quick-drying pigments forced him to paint swiftly. He also liked the sturdy, almost pea-pod shape of the sloop's deep-keeled hull. As he applied an aqua blue wash over the lower edge of the paper, Billy saw himself at the tiller of the Westsail. His surfboard was lashed to the cabin top. He was sailing downwind through a narrow channel, flanked by peeling waves and leaping dolphins, that led into a wide tropical lagoon. On the beach were island girls strumming ukuleles and dancing the tamarae. . . .

"That's fantastic. Do you sell your paintings?" asked a woman's voice with a Southern California accent.

Billy snapped out of his daydreams and looked up at a young couple he judged to be well-financed honeymooners. They were wearing shorts, expensive reverse-print Hawaiian aloha shirts, and slaps. The man had his attention on the surfboard. Her eyes were fixed on the watercolor.

Fighting to keep his cool, Billy smiled and said, "Yeah, sometimes."

"Would you sell that one of the little boat?"

He held the grin and lied, "I usually send them back to the gallery in New York."

He could see she was impressed, but her husband looked skeptical.

"If you were to sell that one, how much would you charge?" she asked.

"Since I won't have to wrap and ship it—air freight's

expensive down here—two hundred and fifty U.S. dollars, if I knew it would have a good home."

The husband switched his gaze from the surfboard and said impatiently, "We've got white walls and a view of the ocean. Is that good enough? How about a hundred in cash, right now?"

"Make it hundred and fifty and you're the owners of a Billy Crawford original."

She looked pleadingly at her guy. He pulled out a fat wallet and began peeling off bills. As Billy opened his Swiss Army knife and sliced the painting off the watercolor block, the husband said, "Nice board. Want to sell it?"

"No way. Where I go, so does my board."

"Searching for the perfect wave, right?"

He didn't like the man's probing and turned his back to pick up a pencil. He signed and dated the watercolor. When they walked off Billy stuffed the money in his wallet and let out a breath. *My first sale. How about that? I'm really an artist now. And thank you, Miss Graham.*

He thought about Miss Graham, his high school art instructor. Without her help and encouragement he probably would have dropped out of high school. *You really made art fun. Hey, I'd better paint another.*

He looked for inspiration and his gaze held on the black-hulled tuna clipper's graceful lines. "She's too industrial for a watercolor, but maybe some crewman would buy a sketch."

He carefully packed the tubes of pigments, his expensive sable brushes that were a gift from his aunt, and a liter bottle of distilled water in his "getaway" bag. Since the near disaster off Bombora, Billy had bought a small waterproof duffel with shoulder straps. He filled it with survival gear and his artist's tools, sketch pad, and watercolor paper. His eyes made a quick inventory of the contents—compass; Swiss Army knife; signal mirror; sunscreen; Mini Maglite with extra batteries; ten granola bars in silver foil wrap; fishing line, lures, and hooks; swim fins; mask and snorkel; and a pair of surfing booties in case he had to walk over a coral reef to reach shore. His prudent organization gave Billy a sense of security. After a long look at the ship he pulled out a number-two pencil and sketch pad to begin drawing the tuna clipper.

The ship's tall knife-edged bow reminded him of a navy destroyer. His sense of form was offended by the wasplike helicopter sitting atop the bridge. He'd leave it out of the sketch, along with the black panel truck parked near the gangplank. The huge mountain of red nylon net on the aft deck seemed appropriate, as did the tall crane that drew in the net. At the very stern perched a broad-beamed, battleship-gray, twenty-four-foot-long skiff used to pull out the net that would encircle the tuna. He would include the skiff as well.

He decided to pencil in as much detail as possible without sacrificing the clipper's graceful lines. Any fisherman interested in buying a drawing would want to recognize the ship he sailed on. "Later," he murmured, "I'll color it with a wash to make it look like a painting, even though that's kind of cheating."

After finishing a draftsmanlike outline he added some shading. He felt stiff from sitting so long. Billy stood, packed his gear, and walked closer to pick up some more details.

He slipped the bag's straps over his shoulders and ambled for the clipper until he found himself in *Lucky Dragon*'s shadow. He paused to look at the truck parked by the clipper's gangplank and saw it was actually a hearse. The boxy truck was a gleaming black Australian Holden, given a touch of color by a pair of silver flower vases attached to the doors, which spouted bouquets of pale red roses.

Billy paused beside the Holden and thought that someone must have died on the ship, and about how near death he and the surfers had been on the paddle back to Bombora. His eyes shifted between the huge clipper and the two sweating Fijian attendants in dark suits waiting beside the open rear doors of the van. He wondered if anyone would have found their bodies if the dolphins hadn't led Druku to them. Billy's musing was interrupted by the large man hovering over him.

"You a boatman?"

Billy turned to look up at the first mate's hairless, blunt head and the scars that crisscrossed his shining skull. He was impressed by the man's larded, muscled body, which would have cause middle-aged wrestling fans in the States to scream with joy.

"Something bothering you, *niño?*" the mate demanded.

Billy composed his response, not wanting to anger the huge tough guy.

"I asked you a question."

"Yeah, I've been around boats a lot. My aunt and uncle— they raised me—owned a boatyard so I grew up with boats. I crewed on a sport fisher and dive boat, ran a surfers' taxi, and worked as deckhand on a lifeguard rescue launch. Yeah, I know boats and outboards, and I can keep 'em running. Why you asking?"

The mate glanced at the clipper and said evenly, "We're short a boatman. Want a job?"

"How long do I have to sign on for?"

"Six months, or until we unload and pay off. Whichever comes first."

"What's the pay?"

"Fifteen hundred a month and a small share of the profits. With our skipper, you'll walk away with three, four thousand extra . . . if you work hard and keep your mouth shut."

"I'll take it. When do I report aboard?"

Before the mate could answer, two crewmen carrying a heavily loaded stretcher struggled down the steep gangplank cursing their heavy burden. Five steps from the bottom, the fisherman gripping the lower end lost his footing and slipped. The thawing body under the blue plastic tarp rolled off the gangplank and hit the dock with a sodden thump.

Billy gasped as he saw the shredded, semifrozen remains of a Fijian. The dead man's skin was lacerated as if raked by jagged meat hooks. One leg was missing at the knee, and the other had been sliced open to the bone. The cadaver looked shrunken and Billy guessed that the man had died from loss of blood, traumatic shock, massive internal hemorrhaging—the works. He shuddered, realizing what had caused the man's death. He turned to the impassive mate and asked, "Shark?"

The man shrugged. "It happens."

As the black-suited attendants hurried to pick up the body, the first mate said, "Collect your gear and report to Captain Gandara." He scratched his bald head as if trying to remember what else needed to be said. "Oh, yeah, welcome aboard *Lucky Dragon*."

CHAPTER FOUR

With his surfboard under one arm, Billy gripped the gangplank railing and bounded up the steep walkway. He was excited and apprehensive. When he reached the main deck he paused and looked about. *Which way to the bridge? And what did the mate say the captain's name was? Gandara. Yeah. Captain Gandara. Sounds Spanish, or Portuguese.*

At the top of the walkway he maneuvered his board so it wouldn't hit the railing. The brittle fiberglass covering the foam core was as fragile as an eggshell. The nine-foot Becker, hand-crafted by one of surfdom's great shapers, had saved his life once, and Billy treated the board with respect.

He walked along the hot steel deck toward the bow. It was time to meet the captain and ensure himself a berth aboard *Lucky Dragon*.

He stuck his head in an open door and discovered the crew's

mess. Several weathered men sat on benches before varnished plywood-topped dining tables drinking beer, coffee, and soda pop. Some read paperbacks with lurid covers that Billy noted had Spanish titles. As he stepped inside and out of the searing heat, his eyes quickly adapted to the dimness. Crewmen gaped at him. A few made little mouth movements that suggested a smile. Most stared blankly. He forced a grin and said, "I'm supposed to report to the captain."

The fishermen sat uncomprehending until Billy asked in halting high school Spanish, *"¿Dónde está el capitán?"*

A thin young man, about Billy's age, stood and moved to face him. He had long, wavy dark hair tied in a ponytail, and wore tight black jeans and a startling white T-shirt with the Grateful Dead rock band logo silk-screened across the chest. He stopped a foot in front of Billy and looked him up and down. He answered with deliberate cool and a challenging grin, "He's on the bridge. You a surfer, dude?"

"I ride some waves."

"Awesome!" he said, mimicking surfer slang.

As Billy turned to leave he gave the Latino kid a raised thumb-and-pinky surfer's shaka salute. Continuing the game, he said, "Thanks, bro."

He climbed the exterior companionway to the wide bridge that projected forward of the enclosed wheelhouse. He saw a deckhand installing huge twenty-power spotting binoculars on a gimbaled mount. Billy walked up to him and said, "I'm to report to Captain Gandara."

The man pointed inside the wheelhouse. Billy carefully placed his surfboard on the deck, and carrying his gear, he entered. Beside the huge first mate stood a bearded man, obviously the captain. He was as tall as Santos but thinner. He had the lean, tense-muscled body of an Olympic fencer. Billy noticed his dark, carefully trimmed beard first. The man's facial hairs were so tightly curled they reminded him of coarse steel wool. As an artist, Billy realized it was the blackness about his lips and chin that made his teeth appear so white. His eyes, in contrast, were light green, almost like a cat's. He wore sharply creased chino trousers, a starched blue work shirt with epaulettes, and low-cut white leather tennis shoes. His nose was sharp and aristocratic. The captain's hands held a parallel rule on a nautical chart. They were large and powerful. Billy imagined them gripping a saber.

Gandara looked up from the map and stared at the new crewman. Then his attention returned to the chart. Billy knew he was facing a man who would take no disrespect from another. Here was a man who had earned, with knife, pistol, and cunning, the right to command *Lucky Dragon*.

As Billy waited, he gazed about the bridge. He was impressed with the vast array of modern electronic gear—GPS receivers, color side-scanning fish-finding sonars, depth sounders, single sideband radios, autopilot, the latest Furuno radar scope, and a weather satellite fax machine. There were more marvels, but Billy's limited experience with large-ship marine electronics kept him from comprehending their purpose. His eyes held on an old magnetic compass in its teak box, mounted before the helmsman's wheel; an archaic reminder that the forces of nature could still be depended on.

The captain stuck a drafting pencil in an electric

sharpener, ground a fine point, and drew a precise line along the rule plotting a course on the chart. He replaced the pencil in the sharpener, turned to the mate, and said, "We'll head northeast out of Suva to here."

Again he honed the pencil point and added a dot on the chart. "About here, we'll send Mr. Lessing aloft for a look-see. It's unlikely he'll spot dolphins this far to the west, but we've been lucky before."

The mate nodded his understanding. With an abrupt movement the captain turned to face Billy.

"Let me have your passport, and then open your pack on the deck," he commanded.

Billy placed his gear on the floor, zipped open the getaway bag, and handed the captain his identification. As the tall man studied the passport, Billy pulled back the flap of his pack. He felt self-conscious about the dirty laundry. To distract the captain he said, "I'm not carrying drugs."

The captain ignored his comment and continued to study the blue passport. He closed the cover and remarked drily, "You have traveled far for one so young. What are you running from?"

"I like to surf. I go where the waves are big."

"So, on your endless summer odyssey."

He touched the pack with the toe of a white tennis shoe, "Everything out."

"Hey, I told you I don't carry drugs," Billy insisted.

Billy saw the mate's scowl and hurried to empty his pack and getaway bag. The captain remarked, "He's an eighteen-year-old innocent, Santos. Forgive him."

The captain scanned Billy's belongings with the detached

expression of a man performing a boring duty. Then Gandara's foot moved to Billy's sketch book. "Hand me that."

Billy picked up the book and offered it to the captain. He turned the pages slowly, inspecting each of the drawings. Billy held his breath, experiencing the same insecurity he had felt when Miss Graham, his art teacher, had critiqued his first portfolio.

"You're a gifted primitive. You should acquire some training," he said softly.

Billy sensed a note of interest that suggested the man might be human after all. "I like to draw. I studied art in high school."

"He's not only innocent, he's educated," the mate said drily.

Gandara's attention returned to the sketch pad. "You have a certain technical skill—keep working at it."

He handed the pad to Billy. "Now, put that small bag on the chart table." He placed his getaway bag before the captain and unloaded the contents. Gandara's long fingers tapped over the compass, granola bars, fishing lures, sunblock, swim fins and mask, signal mirror, and a tiny digital still camera.

"And all this . . . ?"

"My survival gear. I had a boat sink on me once, and had to paddle awhile before I was rescued."

The captain look distressed and said quickly, "No more talk of sinking. It's bad luck."

Gandara tapped the center of the chart with the pencil. "You'll do no swimming or paddling out here. Where I fish, sharks gather."

The captain turned and opened a drawer below the chart

table. He put Billy's little camera inside and said evenly, "This will be returned to you when you leave the ship."

Billy knew it would be stupid to protest and only nodded. Gandara turned to the mate. "Santos, he'll work the seine skiff with Rocha. Now, find Mr. Lessing and have him give our young artist a tour of the ship. And tell Mr. Lessing to explain the rules."

Billy repacked his gear and the captain turned away to open a door at the rear of the bridge. As Gandara stepped through, Billy glanced into the captain's cabin and saw a small dining table set for one with gleaming silver, a crystal wine glass, and a vase of fresh flowers. Against the far wall stood a locked gun rack holding ten automatic assault rifles. On a shelf below the weapons lay dozens of cartridge magazines packed in cloth bandoliers.

As Billy stared at the rifles, Gandara turned and looked at him for a long moment. The younger man wanted to run, but the captain's green eyes held him. "I can feel it when you stare at me from behind my back. Remember that, *niño*, and remember the captain of this ship is your protector and master. If you work hard, and follow orders, your voyage will be uneventful."

Billy was stunned by the man's intensity. For the first time in many years he answered subserviently, "Yes, sir."

The mate led him outside and Billy slowed to run a hand over the spotting binoculars. "Steiners, from Germany. Good optics."

"The best. We have the best of everything. The captain knows quality. He liked your drawings, you could see that."

"Want to buy one?"

The mate's frown shut Billy up, and he followed Santos along the side of the bridge. They stopped where a ladder led upward to the Hughes 300 helicopter strapped to the top of the wheelhouse. Santos bellowed at a small man standing on a red toolbox peering into the open hatch of the engine housing. "Mr. Lessing, the captain wants you to show this kid the boat. You know, fill him in about everything. He'll bunk with you. He's an American, so you can bullshit with him."

Before Santos turned away he grabbed Billy's shoulders. He squeezed hard to make a point and said, "The captain likes you; do not do anything to dishonor him."

"Sure, he's the captain."

"He is our father, and *Lucky Dragon* is our home. You will respect him and work hard."

Billy sensed the mate's intense loyalty and knew any back talk would bring his fist crashing down. He said with a nod that was supposed to convey his sincerity, "I'll pull my share."

"And more, *niño*. You must be prepared to give your life for him. Without the captain, we are nothing."

A voice came down from the helicopter carrying a tone of weary sarcasm, "Ah, come on, Santos. Save your sermon for the Catholics."

The mate looked up at Mr. Lessing and gave him a threatening scowl. The pilot peered down at them and said pleasantly, "Treat me right, Santos, or I might get drunk, crash this beat-up chopper, and miss spotting a pod."

"And you, Mr. Lessing, may a shark piss on your lips."

Santos turned away and walked aft as if he was king of

the deck. Billy watched his muscled bulk vanish and thought, That is one tough dude. No way am I ever going to back talk to him.

"So where are you from, kid?" came a voice from under the helicopter's engine cowling.

"Mostly the Southern California beach scene, but now, nowhere, really."

"Join the club. Come on up."

The pilot closed the engine compartment and reached into a cooler. He handed Billy a sweating can of Coke and popped the top off a beer for himself. "The name's Arnold."

"I'm Billy Crawford. How come the captain and mate call you 'Mr. Lessing'?"

"Gandara honors me as a fellow officer. In the old days I was a captain in the army of the U.S.A."

"And the old days were where?"

He saw Arnold's face cloud. "That's classified."

"Maybe this is an okay question. Why did Gandara go through my gear like a customs inspector?"

"He doesn't allow cameras—still, video, or movie—aboard."

"And he took mine. How come?" Billy asked.

"It's his ship," Lessing added with a cautionary note that chopped Billy's question right there.

Billy took a long pull on the can. "That Gandara, he's an intense guy."

"You might say that."

He sensed that Arnold played it close to the vest and switched the subject. "Must be a real chore keeping a chopper running out here, with the salt corrosion and everything."

The pilot placed a hand on the helicopter's blue-gray cabin siding. The man's touch was one of loving respect for the machine he flew. Billy saw that Arnold's hair was thinning, his hands had a slight tremor, and that there was an eruption of reddish scar tissue around the back of the pilot's neck that the man's sweat-stained T-shirt failed to hide. Then he faced Billy and said, "Damn salt spray eats right through the aluminum if you don't keep after it. And I got no crew chief to pull maintenance. Not like the old days when I only had to fly these birds."

Arnold lashed a canvas cover over the helicopter's forward windshield, and with surprising agility dropped down the ladder to the deck without touching his feet to the rungs. "Let's take a walk, kid."

Billy followed him aft and the pilot remarked, "In port we don't stand watches, except for an engine room guy, the mess crew, and one of the mates. In port he goes easy. At sea, it's different. He's a mean bastard then, and you'd better believe it."

On the way aft the pilot paused below the mainmast that sprouted half a dozen antennae and two radars housed in plastic covers. He pointed up at the enclosed crow's nest and said, "Best place to stay cool in the ship, and about the only place for a little privacy, if you meditate or stuff like that."

"How about all those automatic rifles in the captain's cabin?"

The pilot had had enough of Billy's persistent questions and gruffly answered, "Pirates, Billy, big-time down here."

Arnold indicated the long, thick boom of a crane that was

fixed to the mast, which now lay on the deck. He led Billy to the end of the boom where a giant hydraulic-driven motorized pulley was attached to the top. "That's the power block. It pulls the net out of the water and over the stern so the catch can be untangled and loaded into the freezers. That sucker's so powerful it can haul in a thirty-ton load of tuna, and it has more than once."

They continued aft to pause before a small mountain of red nylon netting. "How long's the net?" Billy asked.

"A little over a mile, and it hangs down from the corkline some three hundred feet deep. It's called a purse seine, because after the catch is encircled, we pull a line that closes the bottom, like closing a string purse."

They climbed the nylon mountain and saw Rocha sitting in the seine skiff with his back to them. The boatman was staring at the sea, unaware of their approach. Arnold went on explaining, "When Gandara orders a set, the skiff drops off the stern and hauls the net out in a circle to trap the tuna. Anyway, Rocha will tell you all about it. His job's running the skiff."

They started down the tangle of webbing and Arnold called out, "Hey, Arthur. Meet your new boatman."

Rocha turned slowly to stare at them. Billy saw a look of sadness on the young man's face and that he had been crying.

"I already met Surfking. I'll check him out on the skiff tomorrow," Rocha said and turned his back.

Arnold pulled Billy away and they climbed back over the net. Billy asked, "What's his problem?"

"He can't go home anymore. What's yours?"

Arnold opened the door to his cabin and waved Billy

inside. He was surprised to find the small, cramped room military-barracks neat. The only adornment was a calendar devoted to old racing planes mounted over the head of the lower bunk. Billy noticed that the bed was made with hospital corners and the thin blanket pulled so tight that a quarter dropped on it would bounce. He remembered that Arnold had been a captain and thought, He's still an officer at heart.

Arnold opened a cupboard and pulled out a bottle of vodka. Inside, half a dozen more stood at attention. The pilot poured a shot for himself and said, "I'd offer you a drink, but this has gotta last." He pointed the glass at the upper bunk. "You're up there, and if you snore, you sleep on the net."

"The captain, is he Spanish or something?"

"Portuguese, out of Mozambique, Africa. His people were big-shot colonials back to the time of Columbus. Would you believe he used to skipper a gunboat? Anyway, then came the revolution, and adios good times and exploiting the blacks. The Gandaras lost everything."

Arnold slugged down the vodka, pulled off his shirt, and turned to brush his teeth. Billy winced as he saw the reddish scar tissue that ran down the pilot's back from neck to waist.

"Burns . . . ?"

The pilot turned to stare at Billy. "You writing a book or something?"

"If you're touchy about it, I'm sorry."

"I went down once and the chopper flamed."

"Come on, Arnold. There has to be more."

"It's X-rated, and you're too young, kid. Now go to sleep. Gandara has the day watch get up at dawn for inspection.

Except for me. Rank has its privileges."

"Inspection?"

"Yeah. He still thinks he's commanding a gunboat."

"What war were you in? Vietnam? CIA in Afghanistan?"

Arnold ignored him, poured another splash of vodka into his glass, and turned his back on Billy.

Billy awoke to the rumbling of the engine and felt vibrations that trembled the steel frame of his narrow bunk. It was pitch black in the cabin, and Billy cautiously eased out of the top bunk to drop silently on the deck. As he groped for the light, he heard a metallic click sound from behind. He found the switch and the dim bulb glowed. Billy turned and saw Arnold propped up on an elbow clutching a .45 Colt automatic. The barrel was pointed at his guts. The pilot's eyes were wide with dread, and the hand that held the gun trembled.

"Hey, Arnold, it's me, Billy," he said soothingly.

He casually uncocked the automatic and slid it under his pillow. "Sorry, kid. I forgot you were here."

"What's going on with you?"

"I dream too much. Not to worry. I've never shot anyone yet. And you'd better report to the mess hall for inspection. If you're late, Santos will kick your butt."

Billy hurried on deck and paused for a moment to look at the first pink tint of sunrise on the eastern horizon. He breathed in the sea air, liking the iodine scent and salty moisture. Then he became conscious that the clipper was moving swiftly. He looked forward and saw its bow cutting a clean furrow through the glassy swells. He felt excitement rising and remembered the one bit of good advice his father had given him, "Never say no to adventure."

He began to think about his dad and the bad times that had split his family apart. It was his father's drinking. After he came back from Iraq he began drinking more and more. The man couldn't stop. *He drank vodka like Arnold. Maybe I shouldn't fly with him. Dad wasn't violent or anything. He just wouldn't admit he was an alcoholic and going wacko.*

He was home when the California Highway Patrol called his mother. She listened quietly, hung up, and told him simply, "He was drunk and ran into a tree. He's dead." He was ten years old when the police called.

The Veterans Administration paid for his dad's funeral. Six months later—six months of feeling like a lost unwanted kid— his mother married one of his father's army buddies. After his third tour in Iraq, Billy's new dad was assigned to Fort Hood, Texas. Mom and his stepfather moved to his new assignment. He didn't want a kid around. . . . *and she left me with her sister and her husband. Aunt Betty and Uncle Al were the best. They really took me in hand.* He remembered their house built over the office of the small boatyard the couple managed and all the lively boaters that came in and out of their lives.

A rough hand clamped down on his shoulder. Billy snapped out of his memories and looked up at Santos.

"Get your ass into the mess, *niño*, or you're going to be late," the mate warned, and Billy hurried after him.

As Billy followed Santos inside, he saw that most of the crew not on duty sat around long wooden tables eating breakfast. Fishermen looked up at him, showing more interest this time. In the serving line, Billy helped himself to coffee, stewed fruit, and eggs scrambled with some sort of dark sausage. At the end of the line stood a tray of bottled condiments with labels that Billy guessed were written in Portuguese. Ahead of him, an old fisherman warned, "Watch out for that hot sauce. It'll burn your guts out."

"Hey, thanks. I appreciate that."

Billy spotted the skiff operator and sat down opposite him. Rocha looked up, and then back at his plate. "Eat your eggs before the speeches, or they'll get cold."

When the captain entered nobody saluted or stood at attention. Instead, conversation ended abruptly, coffee mugs held in midair went back on the mess table, backs straightened and faces became attentive. Billy watched Gandara eye the men and noticed that most of the crew seemed eager for what the captain might say.

The first mate spoke first, "All crew onboard and accounted for, captain. Nobody in sick bay and I haven't had a complaint all morning."

Rocha muttered under his breath, "Who'd dare?"

A short, ruddy-faced man, who spoke with an Australian accent, reported to the captain, "Engine room in order, fuel tanks topped off, and the maintenance schedule is well under way, sir."

The Australian snapped the last out with crisp British military tradition.

"Well done, Mr. McNeal," the captain offered.

A young mate, who Billy guessed was some sort of college-educated technician, stood and described the health of the ship's electronics and that all was well.

"Thank you, Mr. Marusak," the captain responded and turned to face the men. "Does anyone have anything to say this morning? Anything at all. Feel free to speak up."

No one accepted the invitation and Gandara continued, "After we unload at Samoa, we'll be heading for the west coast of Central America. When we start fishing, I want *Lucky Dragon* to be one hundred percent operational. Last night, over the radio, came good news. The price of tuna jumped to sixteen hundred and seventy dollars a ton. That's an all-time high. And I'm sure you know what that means."

The captain swept his eyes across the gathering. "It means," Gandara stressed, "that you can count on an extra two or three thousand above the usual share when I pay off. Work well, honor the ship, and do your duty."

He turned abruptly and left the mess. Santos took the captain's place and said, "That also means you work hard and be thankful God has blessed us with the birds and dolphins to lead us to the tuna. Dismissed."

Rocha stood and looked down at Billy. "You stay here and help clean up. After that, report to the skiff. Understand right now, dude, you do what I tell you, and we get along okay. Got that?"

"Sure. You're the boss. I do what you say."

Benny liked dawn the best. There was always the expectation that the rising sun would bring something new into his life. His senses were fully alive to the sea and the vastness of the pink-tinted sky overhead. Benny's fingers gripped the wheel lightly, feeling every nuance of *Salvador*'s slow, steady passage through the rolling swells.

This dawn, Benny Seeger was a happy man. Last night monitoring the radio, he had picked up a garbled transmission between *Lucky Dragon* and a tuna packer's agent broadcast in some sort of company code. It was clear to Benny that Gandara was heading for Samoa to unload, and then on to the clipper's traditional fishing grounds off Costa Rica. That bit of intelligence would save them weeks, maybe months, of searching.

Sarah appeared next to the captain and handed him a mug of coffee. The rich smell of the filtered brew she had made brought Benny out of his musing and he said, "Not only do you raise money, but you make a hell of a cup of coffee."

"You taught me."

He sipped and moved away from the wide stainless steel wheel. "You take her. Steer zero-three-zero."

Sarah grasped the metal rim and stared into the dawn. Watching the sunrise together was a ritual they had come to enjoy these past weeks at sea. When he had finished his coffee she said, "Benny, you love this old boat, don't you?"

"I guess I do, but I wouldn't be commanding her without you and your dad."

"And the hundreds of people who contributed to the foundation. And if I may, you should be writing your contribution to the foundation's newsletter."

"Oh, yeah, the newsletter. You know what to say. Why don't you write it for me?"

Sarah gave Benny a look of annoyance and thought, Okay, cool it. He's the captain and Benny has lot more to worry about than I do.

She remembered her father's advice before they sailed. "You

grew up in a far different world from Captain Seeger or his crew. You're a privileged child. And your father, he's sort of famous and rich beyond what he ever dreamed he'd be. What I want you to do is remember that on Benny's ship you're no one special. It's like you were drafted into the army. Follow orders, do your job, and you'll have a hell of an experience."

Sarah had replied, "You're saying that my famous dad won't be around to bail me out if I get in trouble."

"Well, I'm glad you got that."

Sarah and the captain watched the sun emerge from a low band of lacy, tropic clouds. Benny's thoughts switched from thinking about Gandara and *Lucky Dragon* to his own vessel. He wondered just how seaworthy *Salvador* really was. The keel had been laid long before Sarah was born.

Salvador was ancient by today's naval standards. She had once been a Canadian Navy minesweeper and had crossed the North Atlantic five times. Her last voyage was from Halifax through the Panama Canal to her final berth north of Vancouver at the torpedo test center near Nanaimo, British Columbia. The navy budget cutters had declared her surplus and the little wooden warship that had never sailed into battle went up for auction. Stripped of military electronics and her single 40 mm cannon, and in need of a refit, the vessel acquired a new owner who tendered the winning bid of 148,000 Canadian dollars.

Benny knew the minesweeper's wooden hull was sound, and her big Cummings diesels would run another 150,000 nautical miles at an honest twelve knots without an overhaul. He considered the vessel a bargain. The Canadian Navy had even left the dishes, galley equipment, and bedding aboard. Benny was pleased with his ship. Though small, and tender in a following sea, she was what he needed. With *Salvador's* bow converted into a sharp stainless-steel-reinforced battering ram, she was a dangerous weapon in Benny's hands. Now, after twenty-seven years of joint Canadian-NATO exercises the ship would at last sail against an unlikely, nonpolitical enemy.

The real foe, Benny had discovered, was public apathy. He needed people's hearts and money, lots of money—money for the Zodiac chase boats and cameras, money to pay for the 5,000 gallons of diesel fuel *Salvador* consumed at sea each month, money to pay for insurance and new radios and a 24-mile–range radar, money for a nationwide mailing to raise more money. And money to fill the freezers and food lockers for a voyage of sixth months. And he would need extra money to make the old minesweeper's bow even stronger, to ram through the steel side of a 268-foot tuna clipper named *Lucky Dragon*. The clipper was out there somewhere in the Pacific and Benny was determined to find and sink her.

He had had just enough money after presenting his cashier's check to the Canadian Navy to sail *Salvador* to Los Angeles. L.A. was where he would find the big donors, if he could create sufficient media interest and produce an "event" to draw movie people and other celebrities to his cause. Enough of them lived along the coast to be familiar with the dolphins who frequently swam, leaping and diving, in front of their Malibu Beach homes. That was where Sarah Thornburg and her movie producer father, Sam, lived. The Thornburgs cared enough to contribute generously to the survival of the dolphins and had supported environmental causes for as long as Sarah could remember.

At the highest tide of the month he had sailed *Salvador* into Marina del Rey yacht harbor. Benny intentionally grounded her on the sandbar at the entrance to the marina. As the tide receded, *Salvador* stuck fast. She would be stranded there inside the harbor until next month's spring tide—time enough for Benny to accomplish his mission.

The harbor patrol, coast guard, and Los Angeles County lifeguards had all screamed he was breaking the law. Benny stalled for time, flew his "Save the Dolphins" banners, invited the media aboard, faced the television news cameras and skeptical reporters from the *Los Angeles Times*, and worked them over as skillfully as a TV pitchman selling miracle potato peelers.

Sarah and her father, Sam, had come aboard to visit during one of his media blitz events. Benny sensed that the girl and her father were appraising him to determine if he was a phony. When the press and camera crews had retired to their laptops and editing rooms, Sam and Sarah stayed and talked with him through the night about saving dolphins. Father and daughter were pragmatic and wanted to help. Sam knew the money-raising game, had the mailing lists and contacts with the movie business folks. He could organize a phone tree, was well-connected to the rich, and believed in Benny's cause. Sarah and her father were a team in every respect. They went to work raising the money Benny needed to send *Salvador* on an odyssey that might lead to losing his ship or, if he succeeded, possibly going to prison for a long time.

Sam and Sarah had good friends among the environmental

organizations and the Hollywood activist crowd, and a very long donor list. Sarah's father created a tax-exempt foundation to support *Salvador* and the money flowed. When all was settled and the sailing date set, Sam had asked one favor of Benny. His daughter was taking a year off to work before starting college with a major in film arts. She wanted to join Benny's crew and sail aboard *Salvador*. Would Benny accept her?

Benny had insisted the voyage could be dangerous, the work hard, and she wouldn't earn a cent.

"It's what she'll learn from you that's important," Sam insisted. "And no amount of money can buy that experience. And besides, she's really good with a camera."

A week later Benny had an eye-to-eye talk with Sarah and asked, "Have you ever been in the water with a wild dolphin?"

"No, but I've studied them, seen them in tanks, touched them at SeaWorld, and felt whatever energy or life force they radiate flow into me. And it's wrong to kill them for profit. That's why I'm here, Benny."

He made up his mind to accept her. "If you promise me one thing, I'll take you swimming with wild dolphins."

"Whatever it is, I promise," she said seriously.

"This is not a game, kid. Or a movie set. You're headstrong and you're your own person. I admire that. But aboard *Salvador*, there's only one captain, and that's me. At sea, you follow my orders. Remember that, and we'll get along just fine."

She agreed, and Benny said, "Okay, you're part of the crew. Between now and when we sail, learn everything you can about seamanship and dolphins."

* * *

It was full daylight now, and she surrendered the wheel. "Your turn, captain. I've got that newsletter to write for you."

Benny gripped the wheel lightly. He liked the feel of the teak deck under his bare, callused feet. He was a seaman first, a crusader next, and a tough guy who knew he could knock out anyone half his age if he had to defend his honor, a girlfriend, or the life of a dolphin. He lost himself in thoughts about his time in the navy until he noticed he was hungry. "Where the hell's that kid who's supposed to relieve me?" he barked at no one in particular.

He glanced over his shoulder and saw Sarah sitting in the deck chair typing on a laptop computer. She was fixed on the screen, and Benny had to bellow to get her attention. "Turn that thing off. Don't you know it's bad for your brain?"

"But, Benny, I'm writing the newsletter for you."

"What newsletter?"

"To your board of directors," she said as if the whole subject pained her.

"What board of directors?"

"The directors of the Dolphin Society. Remember, that's the tax-exempt foundation my dad created to send us out here? Or have you forgotten that the foundation is paying our way?"

"Oh, yeah. The foundation . . ."

She noticed he seemed preoccupied and asked, "What is on your mind today beside mother ocean and dolphins?"

"Fuel, a fouled bottom, a generator that has to be overhauled, and a Portuguese African pirate named Gandara who's heading toward Costa Rica while we're going to Fiji for repairs. That's why we're putting into to Suva, remember?"

CHAPTER FIVE

They stood in the battered gray seine skiff that sat on *Lucky Dragon*'s stern with its aft end pointed downward ready to launch. Rocha explained patiently to Billy, "She's twenty-four feet long, powered by a three-hundred-and-eighty-horse Volvo diesel, and it takes every bit of power she's got to pull the net off the stern."

Rocha leaned forward, and Billy saw him forcing his tough look. The boatman continued, "So after we launch, we go like hell and haul the seine out and around the catch. If we screw up and don't connect the ends fast enough, and the school escapes, Captain Gandara will have my ass. Then I'm going to have yours."

"So, how many fish does that net hold?" Billy asked, knowing that a question would defuse Rocha's L.A.-tough-guy veneer.

"We don't count 'em. We catch 'em by the ton. Last time we fished the ETP—that's 'eastern tropical Pacific'—we made one set that netted twenty-three tons of yellowfin. That was some haul. And those mothers are big. Some weigh two, three hundred pounds. And the freezers only hold about a hundred and sixty tons. It took the guys half a day to brail those tuna."

"Brail?"

"I thought you worked on a fishing boat."

"Where I fished, we caught 'em on hook and line."

"Sport fishing, right? Anyway, brailing is bringing 'em aboard with big scoops, or gaffs, or taking 'em out of the net by hand when it's hauled. That net is a real killer. When it gets pulled in tight—tuna, sharks, turtles, dolphins—everything in it goes crazy, jumping and thrashing, and all the time we gotta keep the net out of the skiff's prop. Look over the stern."

Rocha indicated the skiff's big three-blade propeller and warned Billy never to get near it when the engine was running. He noticed the boat's name painted across the wide transom in Latino graffiti style: YOLANDA.

"Nice name," Billy said. "Your girlfriend's . . . ?"

"None of your business," Rocha said threateningly. "What is it with you that—"

A loud, repeated blast of the clipper's klaxon horn stopped Rocha in midsentence and Billy asked, "What's going on?"

The Latino kid leaped out of the skiff and yelled, "We got an alert, report to your station!"

Rocha sprinted away for the bridge and Billy called after him, "Where's my station?"

Rocha didn't hear and vanished into the superstructure.

The klaxon bleated again and again. Billy wandered toward the bridge, and thought, Are we going to war or something?

He saw men running. In front of him, two seamen pulled a fire hose off its reel and stood by the railing as if to repel boarders. He asked what was happening. One yelled, "Report to your station, on the double!"

He saw movement on the bridge above him. Two men appeared by the railing. One was Rocha, who clutched an automatic rifle and had a bandolier of cartridge magazines slung across his chest. The other scanned the horizon through high-powered binoculars.

Arnold dashed out of the bridge and scrambled up the ladder for the helicopter. He was only a few feet away, and Billy ran for him, calling, "What's happening?"

Arnold paused halfway up and looked down at Billy. "Don't you have a station, kid?"

"I don't even have a life preserver," he shot back.

"Well then, come along for a ride. You're my observer. Let's go. I gotta get airborne right now!"

He followed Arnold up the ladder and was waved into the passenger seat. The pilot pointed to a safety belt and helmet. Billy jammed the plastic dome over his skull and pulled the harness tight across his lap and shoulders.

He watched Arnold flicking switches, readying the helicopter for takeoff, and realized the helmet's earphones were transmitting the pilot's preflight dialog. "*Bluebird* to *Dragon*, we're lighting the power plant. Request you turn into the wind and give me a reading on target direction and speed."

A voice Billy recognized as the first mate's boomed in his

ears, "*Bluebird,* we are turning into the wind. Wind speed six knots out of the southwest. Target about thirty miles north-north-west at zero-niner-zero. Estimated speed, twelve knots."

"Acknowledged, *Dragon.* Up in the air, Junior Birdmen, up in the air we go!"

Billy felt the rotor blades turning overhead—faster and faster—until the cabin shook from the air blasting down on the cockpit. The helicopter's engine screamed to full power. Then, with startling abruptness, the Hughes leaped from the deck. Nose down, the helicopter climbed skyward so rapidly that Billy's stomach sank and his butt was pressed into the seat cushion.

Arnold tapped him and pointed to a binocular case fixed to the passenger side door. Billy drew out the field glasses and moved the tiny microphone that sprouted out of the side of the helmet to his lips. "What am I supposed to be looking for?"

"A small ship that isn't supposed to be out here. Should be dead ahead. The sun's behind us, so they probably won't spot us."

"What's going—"

Arnold reached out, rapped hard on Billy's helmet and put a finger to his lips. He flipped a switch and said, "Now Santos can't hear us talking."

"What's going on, Arnold?"

"A little game called catch the big bad wolf. Gandara isn't liked by some people who don't like the way he fishes. Oh, just in case you haven't figured it out, Billy, we're the pirates. Now put those glasses to work."

Miles ahead, through the binoculars' stereo vision, a small ship appeared, contrasting vividly against the calm, deep blue ocean. Billy noticed that the glasses had a zoom feature and brought the image closer. "It's some kind of old navy ship, could be a minesweeper. Maybe a hundred and twenty feet long."

As they flew closer Arnold asked, "Is she flying any kind of flag, or identifying numbers?"

"Yeah, the American flag!" Billy said with surprise. "And on the bow there's a couple of painted leaping dolphins."

Arnold demanded, "Any Zodiacs on the stern, with big outboards?"

"Two, on davits, like lifeboats." Then he gripped the binoculars tighter and shouted, "And hey, there're women on board."

"Like college girls?" asked Arnold.

"Get closer and I'll give your their measurements."

"Couple minutes more and we should know for sure. Now look for a big guy on the bridge, big chest, big all over."

"Hard to tell . . ."

Billy stared through the lenses. The ten-power magnification brought the images of the man and young woman on the bridge into sharp detail. He was big all right, and deeply tanned. Then his attention held on the young woman and Billy thought, Nice legs and body.

Arnold reached for the binoculars and focused on the ship, at the same time slowing the helicopter until it hovered. "That's him. Benny Seeger. We found him, or he found us. Doesn't really matter. Time to go home."

The chopper banked and flew away. As it did, the rotor blades flashed a momentary reflection. Billy grabbed the glasses and caught a last glimpse of the young woman. *She's really something.*

* * *

From inside *Salvador's* wheelhouse a young man watching the radar scope called through an open window, "Contact, Benny. Some sort of big ship. Range fifteen, sixteen miles out, and heading east at fifteen knots. She'll show off our bow in five minutes."

Benny waved for Sarah and called, "Take the wheel, and right now."

She knew from the tone of his voice it wasn't the time to ask why, and moved quickly to relieve Benny. She noted the compass heading. He grabbed binoculars and with surprising agility for a man so large, raced up a ladder to the top of the bridge. From there he scrambled up the mast that held the radar and radio antennae, then climbed into the lookout's perch. In the crow's nest he peered through the field glasses, scanning the horizon.

He saw nothing but sea and sky. He knew that the radar turning above him would bring in a return farther than the human eye. He also knew that sometimes the eye could beat electronics. He lowered the binoculars and moved his head back and forth allowing his peripheral vision to come into play. At that moment he caught a high bright burst of sunlight reflecting off metal. He lifted the glasses and saw the departing shape of a light blue helicopter. With a cry of surprise he shouted, "Off the bow. Helicopter!"

He leaped for a cable that ran from the mast's crosstree to the deck and slid down to the bridge. Sarah glanced up at Benny, admiring his agility.

Seconds later, Benny took the wheel and sent *Salvador* on a heading after the chopper.

"What's a helicopter doing this far out at sea?" she asked excitedly.

"You're going to college, you figure it out."

He was demanding that she use logic, and Sarah reasoned, "We're about two hundred nautical miles from the nearest land, right?"

"About . . ."

"That's a long way for a helicopter to be out at sea."

"Unless it's on some sort of search and rescue flight, or a military helicopter."

"In that case it wouldn't have flown off. So, let's conclude it came from the ship we picked up on radar. Which means it's a spotter chopper and it could have taken off from a tuna clipper."

The seaman at the radar called again. "That ship's changing course, Benny . . . heading away from us."

"Damn, we've been spotted. Every time we get close, they send up a chopper and haul ass."

He picked up the glasses and studied the ocean again. Far off, where sea met sky, the faint outline of a vessel stood in sharp contrast on the knife-edged horizon. He immediately recognized her rakish bow and the tall steel mast thrusting upward from the aft deck. As he watched the escaping clipper his frustration erupted. "We gotta have a chopper if we're ever going to nail that guy."

She was offended by his harsh tone and said, "Have you any idea what a helicopter, and paying a pilot, will cost?"

"Fund-raising. That's your job, remember? You wanted to see it all for yourself. Okay. When you go back, you tell those candy-ass environmental dilettantes what it's like out here, and why we need a chopper."

He lowered the binoculars and glanced at Sarah. He realized his abrupt response had hurt her. He didn't mean it. Her skin was too thin. With a grin to ease the tension, Benny said mischievously, "It doesn't have to be a new one."

She accepted Benny's peace offering and returned his smile.

He lifted the glasses and studied the ship again. He knew her silhouette from past, fruitless chases that ended with the clipper vanishing into the vastness of the Pacific. Passing the binoculars to Sarah he said, "There she is."

"*Lucky Dragon?*"

"And that's the last you'll see of her in these waters."

"Where's Gandara heading?"

"The clipper's low in the water. That means her freezers are full and they'll be unloading at the Samoa cannery. After that, he'll head for the coast of Central America, probably Costa Rica. That's his usual fishing grounds."

"And we can't intercept him?"

"Not at our speed, and maybe never in this part of the Pacific, now that he knows we're after him. But off Costa Rica, he can be found. And one of these days, I will find him dead in the water with his net out, and believe me, I'll sink his ass."

"Benny, there are laws."

"He's a pirate . . . outside the law. In the old days they'd have blasted his ship out of the water, and hanged him."

"You'd really do it?"

"There are greater laws, Sarah."

"That makes you a pirate, too. Have you thought about that?"

As Arnold descended for the bridge heliport he suddenly aborted the landing to send them climbing high over the clipper. In an excited voice he yelled into the mike, "Got a flock of birds five, six miles off the bow. Could be a school, Santos!"

Billy heard doubt in the mate's voice: "Come on, Mr. Lessing. You've been drinking or something."

"Tell the captain I'm checking 'em out and to get ready to make a set."

Moments later they were flying over a flock of white-winged birds that Billy guessed were seagulls or terns. Below them, misty spouts of vapor shot from the blowholes of several hundred leaping spinner dolphins. Deeper yet, swift-moving fishlike images flashed.

Arnold dove at the pod of dolphins and pointed downward. "See 'em down there below the dolphins, glistening, fat with oil and ready for the cannery. Cannery, hell, we're so close to Samoa we can sell those guys fresh! Big market for fresh or frozen tuna now . . . they sell it as Hawaiian ahi—twenty bucks a pound in Tokyo! Hot damn, Billy boy, you're going see some yellowfin caught today."

He turned away, keyed the radio, and gave Santos the heading. From under his seat Arnold pulled out a beer and popped the tab one-handed. He drained half the can as he brought the chopper down on the landing pad and said, "Dolphin stew tonight, Billy."

"You gotta be kidding."

The pilot ignored his comment, took another swig and said, "I've done my work today, and you, little buddy, are about to start yours."

He jabbed a finger in the direction of the clipper's stern. Billy looked down and saw Rocha standing in the skiff waving them down. "Your San Pedro ex–gang member is waiting for you. And when you get to know him, he's an okay guy."

The chopper touched gently on the bridge and two crewmen sprang to secure metal hold-down clips to the landing skids. As the rotor slowed, Billy called to Arnold, "Thanks for the ride," and jumped out to race for the skiff.

The captain stood beside Santos, who peered through the 20-power Steiner binoculars focusing on the birds that dipped and dove over the fast-moving spinner dolphins. Gandara was surprised to come upon a pod and its associated tuna where none were expected. He was sure now he would order a set, but he wanted the mate to commit himself, so if he was wrong, and the time they wasted was for nothing, he could dump the responsibility on Santos's back. At last the mate looked up and said, "Looks good, captain."

"Are you sure?"

The mate picked up the bridge phone and called the lookout in the crow's nest. "What's it look like to you?"

"It's a so-so pod, and I can see fish below. Tell the captain we got tuna."

"I'm sure, captain," said Santos.

Gandara called into the bridge, "What heading is *Salvador* on now?"

The radar operator answered, "Still north, captain, and

almost off the scope. On a heading for Fiji, I'd guess."

"If she changes direction, let me know immediately."

"Aye, sir."

He considered the problems that would arise if *Salvador* came upon them while making a set. He was tempted to ignore the fish, but they were so close to the cannery, and the price for fresh tuna had never been higher. He made his decision and said calmly, "You may order the set now, Santos. And may God smile on our ship."

The mate reached for a large black button and pressed it three times. The klaxon's insistent blast resounded in every corner of the vessel, sending a shock of anticipation throughout the crew. As the horn's insistent note died, Gandara picked up the bridge phone and turned the switch that would carry his orders over the ship's loudspeakers.

Gandara glanced over the side to watch the dolphins leaping and spinning effortlessly as they raced away from *Lucky Dragon*. Some of the bolder juveniles had forgotten they were being chased and had fallen back to ride the white tumbling wake cascading off *Lucky Dragon*'s bow. He watched them play, admiring their acrobatic grace, and thought, Without you, where would I be?

He turned his eyes from the dolphins, and with the voice of a conquistador ordering his cavalry to slay the unbelievers, he screamed savagely, *"Atún! Atún! Atún!"*

CHAPTER SIX

The klaxon's strident blast, followed by the captain's command booming out of the ship's loudspeakers, energized the crew like a lightning bolt. From every companionway the seamen dashed to fishing stations. Billy was caught up in the frantic rush of fishers dropping chase boats over the side and readying the net for release. He ran on for the stern to find Rocha already in the skiff waving for him.

"So, Surfking's a flyboy now. How come you rate a joyride in the chopper?" Rocha demanded as he hurriedly hooked a line from the bitter end of the net to the skiff's tow bit.

"Hey, he invited me. I didn't have a station, and next thing I knew, I was up in the sky getting airsick."

"You don't look sick to me, bro."

"Just wanted you to know you weren't missing anything, homeboy."

"Enough of that."

"Okay with me. What happens next?"

Rocha checked the pelican hook securing the net to the towline, seemed satisfied it would hold, and said, "It's gonna be a few minutes, or maybe an hour, before we launch. It all depends on how long it takes the cowboys to corral 'em."

"You know a lot about fishing for a—"

Rocha's glare stopped him. "My grandfather was a fisherman. He took me out a lot as a kid."

His attention shifted to the water and Rocha said, "He's going to set for sure."

On either side of *Lucky Dragon* excited fishermen were hurriedly dropping outboard motor-powered speedboats over the side and into the sea. Six of them splashed down, engines roared, and the drivers raced off ahead of the clipper after the pod of leaping dolphins. The lightweight, open chase boats, driven by 125-horsepower Yamahas slammed across the water at 35 knots. The drivers, called cowboys, quickly overtook the dolphins and began to circle the pod. The leaders dove and surfaced, swimming steadily eastward, ignoring the snarling, bucking machines that charged them. Suddenly a geyser of water burst out of the sea in front of the pod, followed by the deep boom of an explosion. Then came more eruptions and another and another loud report. Billy turned to Rocha and asked, "What's that?"

"Seal bombs. When the cowboys can't turn 'em with the boats, they throw those firecrackers."

"Pretty big firecrackers."

"M-80s . . . like little sticks of dynamite. They do the job."

"It's gotta be hard on their ears."

Rocha shrugged and then pointed toward the pod. "Hey, they're turning. We got 'em now. We'll launch any minute."

Billy glanced about the aft deck. Santos and half the crew were standing there. They were tense, like soldiers waiting to charge into battle. Billy climbed on the skiff's engine cover to see better. Off the port side the cowboys were racing around the dolphins that were now gathered in a great mass some 200 yards away. The pod had stopped and the dolphins were darting, jumping, diving, and leaping high to spin and fall back into the sea in a confused, fear-driven frenzy. Then Santos waved at a seaman standing by the skiff's bow. He pulled the pin holding the retaining line. The boat suddenly tipped and slid off the stern to smash into the sea. Billy grabbed the gunwale to keep from going over the side as the big Volvo roared. The skiff surged away from the clipper, hauling out the net that slithered off the stern like a nylon reptile diving into the sea.

Rocha's eyes darted between the pod and the stern of the ship. "Keep watching the net. If it snags, yell like hell!"

They powered out, pulling the net in a huge circle around the confused dolphins. Every few seconds one would leap skyward, spin, and fall back with a splash. Then a tuna shot out of the water and nosed in like a bomb. Already some of the dolphins were ramming into the net trying to force an opening with their beaks. Flukes beat the water into froth, bodies quivered from intense exertion, but the webbing stopped their futile fight to escape.

At the outer edge of the pod the skiff turned and roared back toward the ship to complete the encirclement. Five minutes later the trap was closed and Rocha slowed the engine to idle. They peered over the side and the boatman yelled, "Looking good, Billy!"

"Where are the tuna?"

"Down there deep . . . tons of 'em. You'll see 'em when the net comes in. Man, we're going to be *ricos*!"

Billy leaned over the gunwale and cupped both hands over his eyes to shield the glare. In the lee of the hull, where the boat cast a shadow, he peered through the incredibly clear water. It was almost like looking through a diving mask. Below, a thrashing mix of dolphins and tuna charged about in the wide expanse of net. His gaze shifted along the curtain of mesh where a few of the dolphins had entangled their beaks and fins in the webbing. With a gasp, Billy realized that the ensnared air-breathing dolphins were drowning.

On the bridge the captain turned from watching the net. He was pleased that all had gone well, and with the sea calm and no wind, they would have the catch aboard quickly. He called to the radar operator. "Anything on the scope?"

"All clear."

He picked up the walkie-talkie and keyed the transmit button. "Mr. Santos, you may haul the net."

Out of the speaker the mate's filtered voice inquired, "Will you wish to order a back-down? It's calm. We would release most of them."

"With *Salvador* over the horizon?"

"As you ordered, captain."

In the skiff, Billy and Rocha faced the stern of *Lucky Dragon* watching the net being drawn slowly out of the sea. Sunlight glistened off droplets of water falling from the mesh creating thousands of flashing, diamond-like sparkles. Even from where they drifted Billy could see struggling dolphins and thrashing tuna entangled in the shrinking circumference of the net. Then he caught sight of the sharks, two turtles, and many other trapped fish—the accidental catch that would be discarded when the net was pulled.

Rocha muttered softly, "He's not going to back down. I don't like to see this."

"Back down . . . ?"

"That's when the captain backs the ship up, and revs up the propeller. That causes part of the net to sink so the dolphins can get out. American skippers used to do it all the time. They save almost all of 'em. . . . My grandfather told me about it."

Billy saw that the narrower the net's circumference, the more chaotic the trapped dolphins became. He wondered why they didn't simply jump over the corkline holding up the net. With the slightest effort they would be swimming free.

"Why the hell don't they jump out?" Billy demanded.

"They just don't. I guess it's instinct. They never had a net around 'em till maybe thirty-five years ago, but I heard there's a pod off Mexico that does. The fisherman call them 'The Immortals.'" He saw that Rocha was edgy. "Ach, Billy. Shut the hell up, will you?" The haunted look Billy had seen on Rocha's face when they had discovered him sitting in the skiff crying had returned.

Billy looked across the net which had been drawn into a third of its original size. Nearby a dolphin was attempting to nudge a pup over the corkline. The little creature wouldn't make the leap. Again and again the mother shoved the pup with her beak until Billy screamed at them, "Jump! Jump! Just do it!"

He was furious at the stupidity of the dolphins. A snail could have made it over the net's rim. Without thinking, Billy peeled off his shirt and moved to dive off the skiff. He felt Rocha's hand on his arm and heard him yell, "There are sharks in there. You want to end up in the freezer?"

He looked at the pup. Half its short beak projected over the corkline, and its tail flapped ineffectually as the little dolphin tried to surmount the net. Then Billy twisted out of Rocha's grip and dove off the skiff.

In three strokes he was at the pup's side and hurling the small dolphin over the corkline. He turned to help the mother, but she dove away from him and down the curtain of mesh. Billy peered underwater. In the cauldron of darting tuna and sprinting dolphins he saw the vague outline of the mother in the net. She had jammed a pectoral fin in the webbing and was hanging there seemingly lifeless, as if she had given up the fight to escape. He clawed down the net after her. She was deep and his ears felt the pain of pressure. He pulled apart the nylon strands holding her fin and shoved the dolphin upward. For a moment she drifted, then with a beat of her fluke she shot for the surface to breathe. Billy's need of air was so great he feared he'd black out before making it to the surface.

He burst out of the water beside the dolphin and attempted to shove her out of the net. She was too big and heavy. Billy pushed down on the corkline and then slid a shoulder under the dolphin. "Go on! Your pup's out there!"

With a knee on the corkline he was able to drop the net and at the same time partly lift the dolphin. That was enough to encourage the mother. With a wild beating of her tail, the dolphin escaped the net and swam to her pup.

Billy was exhausted. He treaded water trying to catch his breath and glanced at *Lucky Dragon*. A flash of reflected light caught his attention and he saw the captain peering at him through binoculars.

Something brushed against his shoulder and Billy spun in fright to see a small female dolphin attempting to wriggle over the net. He called to her, "Come on, jump!"

She ceased her struggle and looked at Billy. He was struck by the liquid purity of her eyes. Was she asking for help? He bore down with all his weight on the corkline, sinking it a few inches. The dolphin seemed to understand. Without the slightest hesitation, she wriggled over the barrier. Turning toward Billy, she paused to stare at him. He heard the familiar chattering clicks as she sounded on him, and he reached out to touch her. His movement sent the dolphin leaping away and she fled across the water. He stared at her until Rocha's cry snapped him back. "Billy! Shark!"

He saw the boatman waving frantically for him. Driven by terror, Billy sprinted for the skiff. In seconds he was muscling over the gunwale. Billy stood and looked down. The jaws of a six-foot mako were savaging one of the dolphins trapped in the net. Blood gushed, staining the water, drawing more sharks, and they slashed at the dolphin in a brutal feeding frenzy. Billy felt a surge of rage that dominated reason. He wanted to grab a gun or harpoon, or something deadly, and kill the sharks taking the lives of the dolphins. He turned to Rocha and fought for words to express his feelings. All he could say was "Why?"

The boatman shrugged and turned away to start the engine. Without looking at Billy, he spun the wheel and started back for the clipper. As they floated alongside the clipper, Rocha said, "Now we gotta help unload the net. And Billy, be cool."

They tied off the skiff and climbed a boarding ladder hanging off the aft deck. Halfway up, a loud splash turned Billy's attention to the water. He glanced over his shoulder and saw a dolphin landing in the sea. It was dead and badly mangled. Moments later a shark lunged out of the water and in a single bite devoured half of the dolphin. Billy felt sickened and dizzy. He clung to a rung and fought to keep from throwing up.

Rocha reached for him, pulled Billy over the railing, and led him along the deck. Where the net came cascading down from the power block, a dozen fisherman worked furiously untangling tuna and dolphins from the red nylon webbing.

Dead or alive, the dolphin were untangled and cast over the side to the waiting sharks. The old fisherman from the mess line grabbed Billy and said, "When I get 'em out of the net, you throw them porpoises overboard. They're a little heavy for me, but I can still manage the tuna."

To prove his strength, the old man untangled a young dolphin from the web. It flopped on the deck and her fluke beat against the steel until it abraded and blood flowed.

"Come on, kid. Get it over the side!" he ordered.

Billy hunkered beside the dolphin, wondering if it might survive. There was nothing else he could do but scoop the animal up in his arms and carry it to the railing. He held it over the water and looked down. Sharks were massacring the wounded, half-dead discarded dolphins. Those not visibly injured were so shocked by the trauma of their capture that they couldn't or wouldn't swim to safety. And then there were the babies. Would they survive without their mothers?

"Damn it, drop that sucker and get back here!" the old fisherman bellowed.

Billy looked at the young dolphin he held in his arms and felt her life force course from its dying body through his fingertips and into his consciousness. He murmured, "I'm sorry," and let the creature fall into the sea. At that moment the breakfast of spicy Portuguese sausage and scrambled eggs came gushing out of his stomach and he vomited on the dolphins and sharks below.

He wiped his mouth on his forearm and turned back to the deck to see the captain standing beside the ship's cook. The man in the stained apron held a butcher knife and watched Gandara move among the dolphins littering the deck. The captain paused over a young female that reminded Billy of the one he'd saved and placed the toe of a white tennis shoe on the dolphin. The cook bent over the carcass, slit the throat, and began filleting long strips of flesh from its body.

Billy could only stare and fight down the convulsions that racked him. At that moment, the captain looked away from the dolphin and his eyes held on Billy. He couldn't face Gandara's stare and turned for the railing to throw up again.

CHAPTER SEVEN

That night, as Billy stood in the mess serving line, he sensed the crew's mood was one of tried, cheerful satisfaction. What little he could understand of their talk suggested this was the last set in this part of the Pacific, and the next port of call was Samoa to unload. He turned to Rocha and asked, "How long will we be in Samoa?"

"Maybe three days. Then it's the long haul to Puntarenas, Costa Rica . . . that's home port. We'll fish out of there until we're full and get paid off."

"Then what?"

"We ship out again."

Billy slid his tray along the serving line and waved away some sort of stew the cook's helper offered. He feared what the dark chunks of meat might be and followed Rocha to a table. He noticed that the fishermen on either side lowered their eyes when he looked at them. He had no appetite and could only nibble at a roll. Rocha said quietly, "Not like surfin' out there, is it, bro?"

"You weren't looking too happy either, dude."

Rocha turned away to stare at his plate.

The old fisherman from the net sat beside Billy and refused to look at him. He broke bread into his stew and spooned in the mixture. Billy turned to him and asked, "Is it always that way . . . in the net and on deck?"

The man didn't answer, but continued eating with obvious pleasure. Billy tried again. "Can't some of them be saved?"

The fisherman clanged down his spoon. With a look of annoyance he said loudly, "They're dumb creatures, don't you know that? And didn't God put them porpoises in the sea to catch? And look at us, we're eating the captain's Portuguese stew tonight. You should try it. Good for the stomach."

With an amused, self-satisfied chortle, he lifted the soup plate with both hands and sucked down the remaining sauce.

Billy's stomach tightened. He needed fresh air. As he stood to leave the table he was conscious that everyone was aware of what had happened, but no one would look at him.

The crew's pattern of rejection—the silent treatment—continued as *Lucky Dragon* sailed for Samoa. The mate was even gruffer as he ordered Billy to chip rust and brush red lead primer on the corroding steel. The night before they were scheduled to dock, Billy took his paints on deck and attempted a quick watercolor of a flaming orange-red sunset. Instead of painting the sun, he found the brush moving across the paper, creating flowing images of leaping dolphins. He knew enough about his own inner conflicts to realize he was expressing the pain of his conscience. He dabbed on more paint and added a net to the foreground so the dolphins were jumping over the barrier.

As he worked in the blue wash that represented the sea, he felt someone beside him. Billy looked up and saw Arnold. The pilot stared accusingly at Billy. "You have to face it. They don't jump out."

"And the captain won't give 'em a chance to get out."

"What you did was not smart, Billy. Gandara saw you dive into the net. He doesn't like that. And you know why?"

"Tell me, Arnold. I really want to know. And I want to understand why I've become the ship's pariah!"

"Because you have a conscience, you made them feel guilty. Deep down, unconsciously, they know it isn't right. So you brought guilt aboard . . . and they're going to shut you up for it, or worse. . . ."

"Like the king's messenger."

"It's a war out here."

"And you like war. That's what you did . . . shot people up from your chopper . . . best years of your life, right?"

Billy saw the pain on the pilot's face; an anguish his mask of denial couldn't hide. Arnold turned away to escape Billy's accusation.

"Hey, Arnold. I'm sorry."

He stopped to stare at Billy and said, "It's the only war I've got, Billy. And I'll tell you something about war. If you want to survive, you follow orders and keep your mouth shut."

Billy wanted to mouth back at Arnold. He forced himself

to shut up and thought, Yeah, my dad did that and look what it got him.

Arnold walked away leaving Billy staring down at the dolphins he had painted. The blue wash had run across the paper covering the outline of the net. He ripped the sheet off the block and, with rapid, driven brushstrokes, began painting again.

He was consumed by trying to depict the free, wondrous dolphins that swam in a jumble through his mind and painted on until darkness.

When the mate wasn't after him, and he could find an hour behind a bulkhead out of the wind, Billy painted and sketched dolphins in every possible configuration—ramming a shark, playing with their young, dying in the net, feeding—and in the one he now worked on, with wings and actually flying across the sea.

Where the sun beat warm and nobody watched him, Billy gave his total concentration to the brush, pigments, and paper. He had a sense the dolphins were in control of his brush. Then a shadow fell across the paper and Billy looked up to see the captain studying his work.

"They don't fly, young man. And they won't jump the net."

Gandara's voice sharpened and he added, "I'll tell you only once: no more heroics. There are sharks in the net, as you saw. Stay in the skiff and do your job."

"American skippers saved them," Billy countered.

Billy saw the captain control his anger. Then Gandara sat

on the deck beside him and continued talking as if he were a teacher. "You are young, so I will explain, once. Man has been placed on this earth as master of all the creatures that fly and walk and swim . . . that is God's way. And what God has provided, I will take as is my right."

"There has got to be more respect."

He lifted a hand to stop Billy. "On my vessel, the captain is God, and God gives and takes. While on board, you are my servant. Remember that, Billy, as you draw your little pictures."

He stood and walked off. Billy's hand holding the paintbrush was shaking. His thought about jumping ship until he heard the mate's bellow. "You, the artist. Come over here. I have work for a brush expert."

Santos led him along the upper deck railing that was capped with freshly sanded mahogany. The mate pointed to a plastic container of spar varnish that sat in a bucket of ice, and an expensive pig-bristle paintbrush. "Lay that varnish on like glass. And quickly. It has to be dry by tomorrow."

"Sure, I'll do my best."

"Your very best," he threatened.

"My very best, but chilled varnish takes longer to set up, even in this sun."

"Are you talking back to me?"

He shook his head and ran a finger along the wood, checking for dust. The sanding job was perfect, and he started flowing a smooth, bubble-free coat on the railing.

As Billy worked, he noticed that most of the crew were on deck polishing brass, painting, mopping, and making *Lucky Dragon* glisten. They joked and talked about shore leave, but no one would look at him. He moved the varnish brush skillfully, taking pride in the glistening sheen. He saw Rocha dragging a heavy steel mop bucket and swabbing the deck. As they drew close, Billy said quietly, "Just one question, dude. What's all this cleanup for?"

As Rocha was about to answer, the mate approached and Rocha mopped on to escape. Billy watched Santos pause by the railing a few feet from him and bend over, eyeing the fresh varnish. He sighted down the rail, looking for imperfections, and then ran a finger along the wet surface. Billy couldn't believe the mate would ruin his careful work and shouted, "Hey, Santos. That was perfect!"

The mate shoved his bulk against Billy and wiped the varnish on his finger across the younger man's cheek. "Do it over again, *niño*. And do it right."

"What is it with you? You've been on my back all week!"

Without warning, the mate backhanded Billy across the face and sent him reeling along the wet railing. Santos followed him, his eyes goading Billy to strike back. "Not so perfect now, *niño*. Do it again!"

All the anger and frustration that had been building within Billy erupted, and he screamed, "Go to hell, asshole!"

Santos's fist lashed out. Billy pulled back just in time, and the blow grazed his head. The impact still had enough power to knock him to the deck. Santos kicked at his face. Billy rolled aside and leaped to his feet faster than the mate expected. He hit back and his fist smashed into Santos's nose. Cartilage splintered and blood spurted from his nostrils. The mate roared like a wounded bull, pulled off his wide leather belt, and lashed

Billy. The heavy buckle caught him on the shoulder, opening up a flap of skin. Billy ducked the next blow. Looking for any kind of weapon to drive the mate off, he seized Rocha's mop bucket. As the buckle whipped at his face, Billy hurled the caustic slop at the mate and turned to run. Before Billy could escape, Santos grabbed him and wrapped the belt around his fist like a pair of brass knuckles. As he cocked his arm to strike, Billy did the only thing he could, and jammed a knee deep into the mate's groin.

Deep numbing pain swept through Santos's body and he grew red in the face. The mate was tough, fought through it, and drew his knife. "For that, you're going to die, *niño*."

"Not yet, Santos," the captain said as he put a hand on the mate's arm to restrain his thrust.

The mate backed off like an obedient dog and slipped the knife back into its sheath. Billy retreated and heard Gandara order, "Clean up this mess, *niño*. And you, Santos, make the ship ready to dock."

The captain walked off. Billy snatched the brush and varnish container off the deck and began repairing the mate's damage. He was conscious of the crew watching him. The mate gave him a killing scowl and said, "Do it over, and do it right."

"Anything you say, Mr. Santos."

Taking a chance, Billy turned his back on the mate and began laying on the varnish. After a moment he turned. Santos was gone. He almost fainted from relief.

Deep in the ship's refrigerated fish hold, Billy, Rocha, and half a dozen crewmen worked in the numbing chill, wrapping lines around tuna tail fins, connecting the frozen fish into clusters of fives. On the deck, a stevedore watched for the team leader's signal to raise the load. Then the bundles of fish were attached to a cable and the winch operator pulled them out to be loaded on a waiting Universal Brands cannery flatbed truck. The crew had been in the freezer for two hours and, despite gloves, sweaters, and parkas, the men were freezing cold. A voice called down, "Okay, shift's over. Come on up and thaw out."

The searing, eye-burning Samoan sunshine warmed Billy faster than a hot shower, and in minutes he was sweating. He peeled off his shirt and let the tropic ultraviolet rays bombard his body. He watched several members of the crew walk down the gangplank for shore leave. He wanted to go with them, wanted to call the surf camp manager and beg for his job back. Enough of this, he thought. I've had it. I'm jumping ship tonight.

Billy watched the frozen tuna thump onto the cannery trucks and saw the captain talking with a young man wearing a white sport shirt and jeans. They were standing by a Toyota Land Cruiser with a Universal Brands logo on the door. He recognized the symbol from countless cans and containers he had seen stacked on supermarket shelves. Into his mind came the inane jingle of old television commercials touting Tommy Tuna the dancing fish that leaped out of a net into a white-bread sandwich to be devoured by happy, towheaded children. Billy turned away and walked for the shower thinking, I'm out of here tonight.

His surfboard. That was the problem. He couldn't slide

down a dock line holding it, or dump it over the side because it might drift away in the dark. He had to carry it off. "Maybe they'll all be drunk and won't notice. I'll have to chance it."

He entered Arnold's cabin, began stuffing clothes into his backpack, and had second thoughts about bailing out. His mind chattered on, saying he'd run too often and maybe he should stay aboard until Central America. There were surf camps along the west coast of Costa Rica. Maybe he could find a job. If only he hadn't left the boat to ride those Bombora killer waves.

The door to the cabin opened silently and Arnold stepped inside. He reached for a bottle of vodka and then noticed Billy packing his gear. The pilot poured a drink into a water tumbler. As the bottle clinked on the shelf, Billy jumped with a start and spun. The pilot said accusingly, "Going surfing?"

"I can't stomach what goes on here."

Arnold sipped at the vodka and replied, "Stick it out, Billy. Maybe you'll grow up and get over your illusions."

"What are you running from?"

"Bad things, Billy. But you get over it. . . ."

"With the help of a bottle."

Arnold looked at the glass in his hand and said, "Life's simple. I eat my eggs, follow orders, and fly that rusting chopper. Do your work, Billy, and it'll save you a lot of heartburn."

"I'm getting off, Arnold, before they kill me."

"And run for the rest of your life."

Billy started for the door, turned and said angrily, "Like you?"

Arnold lifted his glass in a peace offering and said, "Touché, Billy."

"See you, Arnold."

"Good luck, kid."

On deck all was quiet. No one stood by the gangplank, and the dock below was deserted. Billy had been standing in a companionway for the past ten minutes watching and listening. Now was the time. Carrying his surfboard and pack, he stepped on deck and moved silently for the walkway. As he reached the ramp a hand shot out of the darkness and gripped his throat.

Billy fought the choking fingers and looked over his shoulder to see Santos grinning at him. Then another hand went around his neck and Billy found himself being lifted off the deck. Hanging in the mate's grasp, he fought for air that wouldn't flow. He dangled, kicking his legs, and felt the life going out of him. Santos shook him like a cat killing a rat. "One thing you do not do to our captain, is jump his ship. If you try it again, I'll feed you to the sharks . . . and to God I make my vow."

Billy felt himself falling. He hit the deck hard and lay crumpled, gasping for breath. He watched Santos walk off. He tried to shout his rage at the mate, but he couldn't utter a sound.

Billy was beginning to hate varnishing, though his skill was impressive. By the last day in port, he had worked his way along the railing and up to the bridge. In an hour he would finish the trim around the wheelhouse windows, and Santos

82

would give him another dirty job. He wiped the sanded wood with a dust cloth and began flowing on a smooth, even coat. Off to the side he watched the captain talking with the young cannery buyer, who carried two large, bulging briefcases. They were close enough so Billy could hear their conversation, and he slowed his brushstrokes to keep within listening distance.

"So how is this crazy American safe-tuna embargo affecting your business?" the captain asked the buyer.

"There's a good chance Congress will lift it. Free trade's a hot item now."

"And you have friends in the government."

"They're for us, but the environmental crazies are fighting to keep the embargo. If it is lifted, the boycotts will start again. If they win, we can still ship tuna in through Taiwan, Thailand, and elsewhere. Then there's the overseas market. It'll be business as usual."

Gandara motioned toward the dock and asked, "And my catch, how does it get to the States?"

"The embargo is only on tuna caught with dolphins. Once it's in the can, who's to know where it came from?"

"And the price, will it remain the same?"

"If there's another boycott, the market may collapse."

"There's always the Asian and European markets."

"We're getting strong resistance from the German Greens. And the French may be next."

"Damn meddling environmentalists," Gandara said hatefully.

The captain noticed Billy watching and ordered, "You, go

down to the galley and bring back something cold to drink. Pronto, *niño*. Pronto."

As Billy turned to leave he heard Gandara tell the buyer, "Let's get out of the sun and begin . . ."

Five minutes later Billy returned to the bridge carrying a tray of iced tea and stepped inside the wheelhouse. He looked around for the captain. A seaman polishing the brass compass housing pointed to Gandara's quarters. Billy knocked softly and announced himself. The captain opened the door and took the tray. As he stepped back to place it on the round dining table, Billy peered inside. His eyes went wide. Before Gandara slammed the door in his face, Billy saw that the table was covered with stacks of U.S. currency and euros, bundled together with wide rubber bands. On the floor stood the buyer's open briefcases. He murmured, "There's a fortune on that table. He must be getting paid in cash. And I bet that's so there's no record of the company buying from Gandara."

He finished his varnishing and escaped to the shade of the aft deck to clean his brush. As he dried the bristles, he thought, There must have been a million dollars sitting there. If a guy could jump ship with that kind of cash . . .

Involuntarily he placed a hand on his throat, remembering Santos. He decided that any attempt to make off with the money would be a very risky caper. He walked to the paint locker and put his tools away. He thought about drawing, then noticed that Arnold was working on the helicopter and climbed up the ladder to help him.

As Billy handed the pilot tools, they talked about keeping the chopper flying without a licensed airframe and engine mechanic. Shoptalk eased the tension between them, and Billy decided to chance a question. "Arnold, what's all that tuna we unloaded worth?"

"He sold a full load . . . sixteen hundred tons, at the current price . . . call it fifteen hundred a ton . . . you figure it out."

He juggled numbers in his mind and came up with a rough total. "That's almost two and a half million dollars. And all that cash was sitting on his table!"

Arnold looked surprised and put down a socket wrench. "What cash?"

"The guy from the cannery was paying the captain in euros and U.S. dollars."

"One way to avoid taxes and keep out of government computers."

"It's because of the embargo. That way nobody can trace where the tuna came from, right?"

Arnold gave Billy a look of warning. "Whatever you saw, or heard, or guess, keep it to yourself. Billy, we're sailing for Costa Rica in the morning. In a few weeks you'll get paid and be off the ship. Remember Arnold's rule?"

"Cover your ass and keep your mouth shut."

"You do that and you'll be around to surf another wave."

He turned, opened the cockpit door, and climbed inside to begin cranking over the engine. Billy called over the noise, "It's all about killing those dolphins to catch tuna, isn't it?"

As the engine fired, Arnold yelled at him, "You keep asking those questions, Billy, and you'll really become the king's messenger."

CHAPTER EIGHT

Benny hated earphones. They were uncomfortable and reminded him of toilet plungers, and they cut off sounds he wanted to hear—*Salvador's* pounding engine, the creaking and groaning of the hull—but he needed to hear what the radio might bring. It was five in the morning, and he yawned.

Despite his left ear's impairment from two burst eardrums, the hearing in his right ear was perfect. Earphones connected to the ship's bank of radios were Benny's far-ranging attempt to learn *Lucky Dragon's* sailing orders. He had been listening and scanning the bands since midnight. At night, single sideband and UHF radio transmissions bounced around between the troposphere and the sea. With any luck he might intercept a message between Gandara and Universal Brands' Samoa cannery transmitter. It had happened before. Benny reached for his coffeepot sitting on a hot plate and poured himself another cup. He knew he should cut down on caffeine, but he had to stay awake.

He adjusted the frequency and scanned the channels. There were so many to monitor—192 in all that *Lucky Dragon* might be receiving or sending on. And the cannery could be transmitting scrambled messages. He knew the company used a code. He'd broken it before, but they had changed it again. Maybe someone would get careless and send an uncoded message. That was what Benny was waiting for: a careless mistake. An hour later he got lucky. It came as a signal bounced erratically from land to sky and down to *Salvador*'s antenna. The voice was very weak. Benny guessed the transmission came from a handheld radio announcing *Lucky Dragon*'s departure to the port captain at Pago Pago. It was a standard, curt transmission from someone on the clipper's bridge followed by the port captain wishing *Lucky Dragon* a safe voyage to Costa Rica.

"Got you now, sucker," Benny muttered as he ripped off the earphones and moved to the chart table.

He unrolled a map of the eastern Pacific and tried to visualize his problem as a whole. At *Lucky Dragon*'s cruising speed, she would take about twelve days to reach Costa Rica. Then Gandara would put in to port for fuel and supplies, probably at Puntarenas. So he'd be fishing somewhere off Central America in about three weeks. Benny shook his head sadly. *And we have to dock at Suva, Fiji, for repairs. How long is that going to take? Maybe a week. Do I chance sailing on with a dirty bottom and a failing generator? We have to fill the fuel tanks anyway. So we make the ship ready, then go after him.*

Benny turned from the chart and spoke to a young

helmsman. "I'm getting some sleep, Jamie. Keep an eye on the radar and depth sounder. We'll be nearing the coast shortly."

Benny entered his cabin, lay on the narrow bunk and tried to relax. Into his mind he brought a favorite image that always helped him fall asleep. He was in the water with the dolphins, somehow given the power to journey with them. His legs kicked like their flukes. Without the slightest effort he could swim at their speed, diving and surfacing, joyously chasing fish. In time, the pod come to acknowledge him as their leader and he guided them safely around the nets. He smiled and then drifted into a deep sleep.

The second day out of Samoa, *Lucky Dragon*'s mast lookout spotted birds working a school of bait and picked up the phone to alert the bridge. The helmsman spun the wheel and sent the clipper on a heading to investigate. Ten minutes later the lookout put down his binoculars and reported dolphins under the wheeling, dipping flock.

The captain studied the pod through spotting glasses. It was a large throng and the schooling yellowfin below the dolphins would number in the thousands. Gandara turned to Santos. "Unusual to find them out here so far from land. Perhaps it's the currents, or the seas are growing warmer. Something's changing their migration pattern."

"It's because we have a lucky ship," Santos said, grinning with anticipation. "And we will find tuna with them. I can feel it, captain."

"So can I, Santos. Shall we gamble and make a set?"

"With you, the odds are good."

Gandara called into the wheelhouse, "Radar?"

"Nothing on the scope, captain."

Gandara patted Santos on the back like an Englishman petting his pet Yorkshire terrier and said, "This time, Santos, you order the set."

The mate smiled, tapped the klaxon's button, and picked up the mike. *"Atún! Atún! Atún!"*

Billy's stomach constricted as the skiff dropped off the stern and smashed into the water. He didn't want to be in the boat, but Rocha had grabbed him and hurled him aboard with a warning that his refusal to work would give Santos an excuse to belt him again. Remembering the mate's hands around his throat, Billy stood numbly and watched the net spill off the clipper's stern. He knew enough now not to ask about the sharp thump of the seal bombs exploding in front of the pod that destroyed their acute sensing capabilities. The sight of the cowboys harassing the dolphins ignited his anger.

He turned to Rocha. "It's like we're at war with them. There's gotta be a better way to catch tuna!"

"Yeah, with hooks, like my grandfather used to use. In the old days, they'd throw bait in for 'em, then cast out the hooks. Tuna bite on anything. He said they caught one-, two-, and three-pole tuna."

"What's that mean?" Billy asked, wanting to keep the talk going.

"Small tuna . . . one man to one pole and a hook. Bigger tuna . . . two men to two poles and a line to one hook. And for the big ones, it took three guys holding three poles attached to one line and a single hook. Yeah, they'd catch a few hundred out of a school. Big deal. With the net, we get 'em by the thousands."

They stood in the roaring skiff listening to radio chatter between the bridge and the chase boat drivers. Billy bit his lip and prayed the dolphins would not be stopped by the cowboys hurling seal bombs. The voices from the speaker were excited, anxious, and Billy heard one of the cowboys yelling, "They're not turning. There's a big male leading them away! We're losing 'em!"

Then Gandara ordered, "Well then, stop him."

"Jesus, captain, how?"

"You're a boat driver, aren't you? Chop him up with your propeller."

As they raced to close the net, Billy saw one of the speedboats charge the lead dolphin. The snarling outboard was no more than thirty yards away when it rammed into the big male. An instant later the propeller sliced through the creature's back, ripping him open to the spine. His murder stopped the old dolphin's followers and they turned aside to group around him. Several of the pod nudged him with their beaks as if mourning his death. Rocha drove the skiff around the milling, confused dolphins, and the net sealed off their escape.

Billy turned his eyes away and peered over the side looking for sharks amid the cauldron of thrashing creatures. Maybe this time there wouldn't be any. Maybe the captain would order a back-down. He shifted his eyes to the sea. It was oily calm, without a cloud in the sky. Rocha had said that in smooth seas American skippers always backed down, allowing almost all of the dolphins to escape the net. It was during night fishing, or when the ocean was rough, Rocha had explained, that disaster sets occurred. *Well, today, damn it to hell, it's like a swimming pool out here.*

Rocha yelled for Billy to cast off from the net. He reached over the stern and unhooked the line. Then Rocha turned the skiff away from the clipper and they idled alongside the cork-line, some fifty yards off *Lucky Dragon's* stern.

As the net drew tighter, the frenzied dolphins beat against the mesh and became entangled, drowning themselves. Billy yelled at Rocha, "We gotta cut the net!"

"Are you crazy or something?"

"Don't you understand? We gotta save them!"

"Shut the hell up!"

Directly below the corkline a dolphin struggled in the webbing, drowning before Billy's eyes. His rage came pouring out. He jumped on the engine cover and screamed, "Damn you, you're killing them all, you bastard!"

On the bridge, Gandara leaned against the railing watching the seine skiff when Billy's cry reached across the water. The captain swore and lifted the binoculars hanging around his neck. He focused on the skiff and saw the young American dive into the net. Gandara murmured, "Since you like to swim so much . . ."

Amid the thrashing, crazed dolphins Billy dove and untangled one. Riding it to the surface, he thrust it over the net. Another beat against the corkline, and he hurled it over the rim. He was consumed by his battle to save them and lost all sense of where he was, who he was, what he was. All that mattered was freeing them. He failed to realize that the net was shrinking around him until he heard Rocha yell that sharks were arriving.

His hands went around the body of a small female caught in the upper strands. At his touch she ceased struggling and allowed him to untangle her. She looked familiar. He thought the dolphin might be one he had saved before and began swimming her toward the corkline. As he gasped for breath, he told the dolphin, "Not so smart to get caught again."

On the bridge, Gandara picked up a handheld radio and keyed the transmit button. "Rocha, bring the skiff back immediately, and I mean right now."

The boatman's astonished voice came out of the radio's tinny speaker. "But, captain, he's—"

"Now, Rocha! That is an order! Pronto! Pronto! Or you're shark bait too!"

He saw the boatman hesitate, then start the engine and turn the skiff toward *Lucky Dragon*. Gandara turned to yell at the helmsman, "We're getting under way. Give me three knots, slow and steady."

He brought the radio to his lips, "Santos, haul the net as fast as you can. Pronto, man. Pronto!"

Santos didn't question the command.

Billy reached the corkline and gently shoved the little female out of the net. The dolphin floated just beyond the rim, looking at him instead of swimming away. Billy called to her. "What's a matter with you?"

He wriggled over the net and reached for the dolphin. This time she didn't swim off. He put his hands around the dolphin's body and began to tow her from the net. As they inched away from the corkline she drew life from his touch. He felt her quiver. Then her fluke began to beat against the water. "Go on," he urged. "You can make it. Get out of here!"

The dolphin gathered strength. With an energetic beat of her tail, she swam on. He watched her leave and turned to look for the skiff. The boat wasn't there. He spun toward the ship. His eyes went wide with dread. The skiff floated beside the ship and the net was being drawn aboard.

He screamed at the clipper, "No!"

On the aft deck, Rocha heard Billy's frantic cry. He turned to see the captain on the bridge wing watching Billy. Santos moved quickly to intercept Rocha and grabbed the boatman. "Stay out of it, *niño*. . . ."

In the water Billy sprinted after the trailing edge of the net that retreated from his grasp. He swam harder and faster, faster than when he had won the lifeguard one-mile rough water swim two years ago. But he wasn't fast enough to seize the corkline.

He gave up and screamed at the departing ship, "Don't leave me!"

The crew turned their backs on him and returned to work. Only Rocha remained at the railing, staring at him with a haunted expression of resignation.

Billy's chest burned from exertion and he was forced to tread water. As the ship sailed off he saw Gandara and Santos move toward the midship railing. A splash of bright color caught his attention. The mate was carrying his surfboard, and he saw Santos throw it far over the side. A moment later he hurled Billy's pack and getaway bag into the sea, removing the last evidence of his existence. Billy realized that by disposing of him and his things, Gandara was cleansing the ship of the guilt he had brought aboard.

Exhausted, and badly frightened, Billy watched the clipper sail away. There was nothing he could do except swim for the surfboard and climb on. As *Lucky Dragon* receded from view, the last of the dolphins caught in the net were tossed overboard leaving a bloody trail of their dead and broken bodies in the clipper's wake.

With tears of fear, rage, and frustration streaming down his face, Billy sat up straight and bellowed his outrage, "I'll sink you, Gandara, I swear to God I will!"

Emotionally drained and physically exhausted, Billy turned away from the ship and looked about. There was nothing to break the empty line of horizon.

CHAPTER NINE

Tears and anger gave way to thoughts of his impending death. After that, the desire to survive overcame his sense of hopelessness.

Billy thought, How far am I from land? We were a day and a half out of Samoa, maybe two hundred miles from the coast. Which way? Yeah, it has to be southwest. With water and food I could paddle twenty-five miles a day. That's eight days of paddling. I can catch fish, maybe. But without water, I'm dead.

He took two strokes and sent the surfboard gliding ahead to retrieve his pack and getaway bag. He cursed Gandara and Santos for giving him the means to prolong his agony. And it's going be agony, he thought. Am I kidding myself? I might as well end it now. How? Dive down a hundred feet and suck in a gallon of seawater? Hang myself with the surf leash?

Billy set his two packs on the deck of his surfboard and

opened the larger one. He began tossing aside things he wouldn't need. Into the water went Levi's, T-shirts, shorts, jogging shoes, his leather shaving kit. He'd keep the nylon wind shirt surfers wore to help prevent paddling rash. Good-bye to all the rest. His earthly possessions drifted away and sank. He opened the getaway bag and began an inventory. Here were treasures that would mean life or death, and he laid them on the surfboard's deck. He picked up the compass and took a sight. The needle quivered and settled on its northerly magnetic point. He turned the bezel and hoped he had the right direction to Samoa. The fishhooks, line, and lures were critical, as were the sunscreen and nylon wind shirt. The twenty-foot length of stout nylon line would come in handy. He wiped a drop of water off his stainless-steel signal mirror and polished it. The mirror's glint reflecting in the eyes of a sleepy lookout could save him.

There was also food, and he said aloud, "Ah, granola bars. Ten of 'em. I'll catch fish and eat one granola bar a day. Ugh." Then his fingers caressed the quart bottle of distilled water he used for his watercolors. He was thirsty already. *Two swallows a day, and chew some raw fish for extra moisture. Hey, I'm gonna make it.*

He was tempted to discard his paints, brushes, pencils, and sketch pad. But his artist's tools meant too much, and he stuffed them back into the waterproof bag. He still had his wallet, his passport, and the money from his first watercolor sale. He pulled the soggy billfold out of his shorts and packed it away with the rest.

The day's last minutes of sun still gave a radiant warmth.

He knew in the nights to come he'd suffer from the cold, and with daylight he would curse the endless, searing, body-blistering heat, but for now the sun was a comfort.

"I'll make it!" he screamed at the fiery red ball as it touched the western horizon. "And I'll see you in hell, Gandara!"

He began paddling. One hundred strokes, than a two-minute rest. He alternated between paddling prone and on his knees. He stroked on and on until total darkness and a million times a million stars shone overhead. The physical effort kept him sane and partly stilled the fear that surged in his guts. He was dancing on the edge of panic. One hundred strokes. Rest. Look at the stars. Ask how they got there. Then one hundred more. When the Southern Cross appeared he stopped and pulled on his tightly woven nylon wind shirt. Next he reached for the safety leash that surfers use to connect themselves to their boards. His was ten feet long, incredibly strong, and elastic. He had gone over the falls many times in twenty-foot waves and had seen the leash stretch to double its length. Each end had a loop of adhesive Velcro. The loops allowed one end of the urethane cord to be secured to a ring in the tail of the board. The other end was strapped around an ankle. He fixed the leash to the board and his leg. No matter what happened during the night he would stay connected. Without the board, he was dead.

Billy leaned forward and lay on the surfboard. Keeping movement to a minimum, he cradled his arms around the getaway bag and began taking deep, relaxing breaths. His body unconsciously adjusted to the tipping and tilting of the board, and the water that sloshed over his elbows and feet. In less than a minute he fell into a fitful sleep.

He awoke at dawn and sensed that something off to his left was watching him. He sat up, stiff and sore, and moved his aching shoulders. His eyes roved across the sea. Nothing was out there except the tint of dawn rising in the east. Not a cloud in sight. No chance of a squall to drench him with rain. Not even a bird. He thought, One sip of water now, then I'll try fishing.

Billy carefully broke the plastic bottle's seal and unscrewed the cap. Taking great care not to spill a drop, he put the lid into a pocket. To lose the cap, and not be able to contain the quart of water, would be a disaster. He brought the bottle to his lips, and fighting to keep from draining it all, filled his mouth. He rinsed the liquid around, savoring it, and then slowly swallowed. He carefully replaced the cap and stowed it back in the bag. Next, he tied a wriggly plastic trolling lure, with its sharp barbed hook, to a length of fishing line and let it out a hundred feet. He secured the line to the loop at the end of the surfboard leash, figuring if he hooked a big fish the elastic cord would take the shock. Next he cut off two feet of nylon line, made a lanyard for his Swiss Army knife, and hung it around his neck. If he did catch a fish, he would have to kill it quickly or chance being thrown off his board. If the fish was really big, he'd have to cut the line or be yanked off his surfboard. That was his big fear. Losing his board meant it would all be over. He began paddling again and glanced back. The brightly colored lure skipped across the surface and Billy muttered, "If I were a fish, I'd sure take a bite at that."

Then he saw a flick of movement far behind the lure.

Something surfaced, and then disappeared below the water. Billy held his breath. *Let it be a small tuna. No more than twenty pounds. If a shark hits it, there goes my lure. Come on, tuna. Bite!*

Nothing happened. He paddled on, towing the dancing plastic wiggly as the sun climbed higher. Billy stopped to rest, slathered lotion on his tender nose and reddened face, then coated the backs of his legs where he was already starting to burn. Out of the corner of his eye he saw something dark move. He saw it again—the tip of a black dorsal fin. Then it was gone. Was it a great white, a mako, a tiger? It wasn't after his lure. Was it after him? At noon, with the sun hammering down, he ripped open a granola bar and wished he'd packed canned pineapple instead. The dried fruit and abrasive grains didn't produce the saliva he needed to swallow. He was forced to take a gulp of his precious water to get the concoction down. He capped the bottle and reached for the sunblock to put another layer on his nose. As Billy lifted the tube out the bag he saw a shadowy barrel-shaped form swim swiftly under his surfboard. Startled, Billy dropped the tube and yanked his legs out of the water. "What the hell was that?" he muttered fearfully.

He knew that whatever it was had been following him. Then he noticed that the tube of sunscreen had floated away during his moment of fright.

His eyes searched the water for the bright plastic container. Nothing. It must have sunk, he thought bitterly.

He was burning up and had to cool off. He stared underwater for several minutes. There was nothing but blueness fading to gray and he chanced sliding off the board. He hung there with his arms across the deck, allowing the water to ease the pain of his sunburned legs. He peered underwater again. It was as peaceful as before. *I'll rest a few moments and then get going.*

He laid his head on the surfboard and closed his eyes to shield them from the glare. With his body supported by the buoyancy of the salt water, Billy drifted into a momentary half-sleep, half-daydream of floating down a freshwater river in a bouncing inner tube. He saw himself scooping up the clear, chill mountain water and drinking his fill. His mind shifted to the day he had moved in with his Aunt Betty and her husband, Al. He had been ten years old, and from that day on, his life abruptly changed for the better.

Betty and Al owned a small but successful boatyard in a large Southern California marina. Along with the love they gave Billy, they put him to work, and he quickly learned how to maintain and operate pleasure boats. His newfound skills led to paid work around boats. School friends ignited his interest in surfing and competitive swimming. Billy remembered with pride passing the beach lifeguard one-mile rough water swim test and his promotion to deckhand on a rescue launch. After high school he spent his entire savings from his boatyard work for a plane ticket to Fiji and a monthlong stay at Bombora Surf Camp. His ability to run small boats and repair outboard motors landed him a surf taxi operator's job. With a resigned shake of his head he remembered how he'd screwed up and lost the best job a surfer could have.

He began feeling sorry for himself and thought, Betty and Al, they gave me a lot of freedom and confidence. Maybe too much. Maybe I wouldn't be floating out here now if they'd been more protective. Come on. Get real. It's not because of them I was abandoned.

Fighting to stay awake, he tried to remember all the boats he had ever sailed on. There had been a lot, but they were a jumble in his mind. His thoughts were so scattered by a constant nagging thirst and painful sunburn that he couldn't concentrate. What he did recall was that every boat he'd been aboard had an ice chest or refrigerator loaded with cold fruit juices and soft drinks. He imagined reaching for a bottle of chilled lemon-lime soda, twisting the cap off, and drinking it down until he burped.

Relaxing in a haze of good memories about Betty and Al and fun times surfing, he started to fall asleep. Then suddenly a nearby movement of something dark jolted him fully awake. Whatever it was came again, right for his legs, and then passed beneath him. He scrambled back onto the surfboard and looked wildly about. The sea was empty and he thought, It's playing with me, like I'm its toy.

Something hit him on the head. Before he could cry out, the tube of sunscreen landed on the board. It had been punctured and was oozing lotion. "What the hell?"

He spun and saw a dolphin rise out of the water. A dab of white lotion by its mouth told him who had thrown the tube. As the small spinner chattered at Billy, his fear subsided and he called, "Look what you did to my sunscreen."

The sound of his parched, gravelly voice startled him, as it did the small dolphin, who dove to swim under his board. He called after it, "Hey, come back."

The dolphin surfaced again, closer now, almost within Billy's reach. He didn't dare make a motion that might frighten it away. He studied this curious mammal, with its anatomically fixed grin. It was a female, and she looked familiar. Her rapid clicks and high-pitched squeaks came again. Billy looked closer and saw abrasions where the dolphin's beak projected from her head and thought, She's the same one I freed from the net. And I got you out twice, didn't I?

He chanced a soft whisper. "Hey, you know me. I saved you from Gandara."

She chattered again, and Billy asked, "So what are you doing following me?"

The dolphin swam a few inches closer and sounded a new, slower vocalization that Billy guessed might mean she was more relaxed with him. He sank to his knees and began to paddle, hoping the dolphin would stay abreast of him. She swam alongside, and he continued the one-sided conversation. "Okay, I've heard the stories about dolphins pushing people lost at sea to shore. Your kind saved my life, so I'll believe anything. But you're playing with me, right? You're all alone out here and you're bored. And what about the guys you push the wrong way? We never hear from them, right? Well, I'm not going to be much fun for you."

Then he realized the dolphin hadn't joined him for fun and games. "Your pod, your whole family, they died in that net, didn't they? You're all alone like I am. Did you come to adopt me? Or have me adopt you? A lot of good I'll do you. And I'm sorry for what happened; I want you to know I had nothing to do with it."

He smacked the side of his head with the palm of his hand and thought, Talking to a dolphin like this—the sun's getting to me.

The dolphin came closer, and he reached out to run his hand over the top of her head. She didn't pull away, and he felt her energy flow into his fingertips. For the moment, his loneliness eased.

Right now, at his side, another living creature was sharing his pain. He desperately needed the dolphin's companionship and had to hold himself back from hugging her. He remembered seeing the *Flipper* TV show as a kid and said aloud, "You're not Flipper. Flipper always had a happy ending. He never died in a tuna net. Flipper used to save Bud and Sandy, and next week they'd save him. How about saving me?"

She nudged his surfboard and he asked, "What's your name. Click-Click? Big Beak? Chatter? Hey, that's good. Mind if I call you Chatter? Do you understand? I'm a mammal like you. I nursed at my mother's breasts, and females of my species give live birth like your kind. But I have to have water without salt. And how about some raisin bread with almond butter and bananas? You know, health food stuff."

With a cry of desperation he yelled at the dolphin, "But I'd settle for a gallon of fresh water. Can you do that?"

At the rising of his voice, the dolphin leaped over the surfboard and vanished into the depths. He told himself, My mind's going, and I've only been out here one day. You're supposed to be tough. So get with it, Billy. You're not dead yet.

He looked for the dolphin, but she had gone, and he

thought, My life's going to end on this ocean feeding the sharks. And what did I ever do for anyone but myself?

To still his fears, Billy began paddling furiously, hoping the physical effort might bring back some sort of sanity. When his shoulders stiffened he came to his knees and kept on. An hour later, exhaustion forced him to stop, and he collapsed on the surfboard. He lay on the deck gasping, fully aware that the sun was blistering the backs of his legs and dehydrating his already parched body.

He rolled off the board to cool down. He heard her click-tick-clicking at him, and a second later she appeared at his side. He felt a surge of happiness. He wasn't alone after all. As Billy climbed back on the board the dolphin surfaced next to him. He saw she was holding a limp and lifeless fish in her mouth and suppressed a shout of joy. He spoke to her calmly so she wouldn't drop the small tuna.

"That's a beautiful fish, Chatter. Did you catch it for me?"

She moved next to Billy and he slowly reached for the fish. Taking it by the tail, he give it a little tug and said, "Really a great-looking fish. Now let it go, and we'll share . . . fifty-fifty, okay?"

She wouldn't release the fish and Billy felt a moment of panic. He stroked Chatter's head and his touch seemed to relax the dolphin's jaw. She dropped the fish and it fell into the sea. As his heart skipped a beat, Billy snatched the fish and laid it on the surfboard. He flipped the big blade out of his Swiss Army knife and began to fillet the tuna. "Really a nice fish, Chatter. How'd you know I like sashimi?"

He handed the first strip of the firm, moist flesh to the

dolphin. She accepted his offering and it went down her throat. He popped a chunk into his mouth and chewed. "This is awesome. I bet there's a cup of water in every pound."

By the time the small tuna was nothing but viscera and bone and the liver, which he couldn't bring himself to swallow, his stomach was full. He stroked the dolphin, sensing she liked his touch. "Here's the idea, Chatter. I pet you, you catch fish."

He gave her the liver and rubbed her head again. "I pet, you bring fish. Got it?"

She shook her head energetically and squeaked at him.

"Does that mean yes, or no, Chatter?"

He stared at the dolphin and thought, If she brings me another one, that means I got through to her. If not, I'd better learn to speak dolphin, and fast.

Feeling refreshed, Billy paddled on until fatigue forced him to rest. He pulled in the fishing line, and the useless lure, and connected the leash to his ankle. As he fastened the Velcro strap he thought, Maybe with Chatter, I have a chance.

CHAPTER TEN

Three days later Billy held the water bottle high and drained the last few drops into his mouth. The jug was empty, and with it went his confidence that he might survive. His will to live was evaporating as rapidly as his body was drying out, and he tossed the plastic bottle aside. Chatter discovered the buoyant jug, a fascinating plaything, and kept bringing it back to Billy. He'd throw it away, she'd bring it back. They evolved a game, but the water bottle always came back empty. Though the dolphin had brought him two more fish, Billy knew he was suffering from dehydration. He searched the horizon hoping to see a rain-pregnant squall come boiling out of the south to dump rainwater on him. He paddled on thinking, Maybe she wants me to keep the bottle. Maybe she's teaching me, and I'm not smart enough to understand her.

Late on the fourth day Billy noticed sores on his ankles and hands from their constant immersion in salt water. And the meager intake of fish flesh was certainly adding to his body's absorption of salt. When he brought his fingers and feet out of the water they hurt painfully. He began to dream of rolling in the snow and stuffing his mouth with the icy-cold white stuff. Then came memories of turning on the water spigot in his parents' kitchen and sticking his mouth under the faucet to drink his fill of chlorine-contaminated Los Angeles County tap water. *It was a crummy kitchen, but there was always something to eat, even if it was Hamburger Helper. God, I'd like a cold pineapple smoothie. Oh, shut up and keep going.*

He paddled into another flaming sunset. With abrupt swiftness night came, and Billy was plunged into darkness. He felt a change in the weather. It was colder. He paddled on, sighting between his compass and the Southern Cross. Then a chill breeze came out of the south and he began to shiver. "All I need to make life perfect is a hurricane, or do they call them cyclones south of the equator?"

He stroked on through the night, occasionally glancing into the darkness to check on the dolphin. She was there, swimming steadily beside him. Chatter was a comfort. He knew he would have freaked out days ago without her at his side.

He tried to sleep on the board, but the breeze was causing it to pitch, and it was impossible to stretch out. Sometime before dawn, despite the chill, Billy's head sagged and he slept fitfully until he felt Chatter's beak nudging him.

He opened his eyes and saw a dark squall line on the horizon. At first he thought he was hallucinating. He took a deep breath and pinched an earlobe. He was awake, and the sea-hugging clouds seemed to be moving closer. When a moist wind kicked up whitecaps, he allowed his hopes to soar. "It's going to rain, but is it going to rain on me?"

As the storm front rolled toward Billy, he stopped paddling, ripped off his wind shirt, and made ready to use the tightly woven cloth to catch the rain. He was glad now that Chatter had forced him to keep the bottle, and if he was careful, he could funnel any water he caught into the narrow top.

The first drops were cooling little caresses that washed away the encrusted salt. Like a sponge, Billy's parched skin soaked up the moisture. As the downpour grew in intensity he held the nylon cloth out to catch the rain. Then the sky turned black and fresh water fell in torrents. There was no horizon, no sea, no sky. Only the fresh, cold water raining down. The marble-size drops battered him painfully, but their wet sting meant life.

The wind shirt filled in seconds. He pressed his lips into the water and sucked in his fill. When he could drink no more, he tilted the corner of the cloth to the opening of the bottle. Water flowed into the container so quickly it filled in a minute. He screwed the lid back on and looked about for the dolphin. Chatter's head was out of the water and she floated with her mouth open catching the raindrops. He called to her over the spattering noise, "Thanks for bringing the bottle back. Did you know it was going to rain?"

The squall raced on and moments later the sun beat down so hot that the droplets on his board steamed as they evaporated. As he paddled on, he talked with the dolphin, trying to teach her his name, and the name he had given her. She responded when he called, "Chatter." Or was she reacting to the sound of his voice rather than the name? He knew that when he slept she stayed close to him. When his touch was soothing and given with love, the dolphin would nudge him back. Billy realized there was some sort of strange empathetic communication evolving between them and he thought, We're together twenty-four hours every day. If we didn't pick up clues about each other, we'd be nothing but driftwood.

The constant paddling was draining his strength. He could no longer take a hundred strokes between rest breaks. It was down to twenty, and it took him ten minutes to recover from the effort. He glanced at Chatter and said, "I'm going to need some help, and you're going to learn a new trick. It's called tugboat. You're the tug and I'm the boat."

Billy's eyes flicked from the leash fastened to his ankle to the other end, which was attached to a loop of nylon cord tied to a fastener embedded in the fiberglass and foam at the stern of his surfboard. He realized that if Chatter could be taught to tow him, he had to fasten the surf leash to the bow. He could solve that problem, but it would mean boring a hole through the fiberglass at the nose of the board and then threading a nylon fishing line through the opening. The opening would allow water to seep into the foam core, which would ultimately rot the surfboard. *But, what the hell? It's my life. Becker can always shape me another board.*

With the awl of his Swiss Army knife he drilled a narrow hole through the board's nose, inserted the line, tied a loop, and then attached the Velcro end of the surf leash. "If we're gentle with this it should hold. Okay, Chatter. Let's play tugboat."

He freed the surf leash from his ankle and flicked the looped end at Chatter. She was immediately interested in the new game and flipped the leash back at him.

As she came close, he again dropped the loop over her beak and made soothing, happy sounds. She cast it aside easily, but came back again and again to have Billy drop it over her beak. She couldn't get the idea of towing him. He fought down his frustration and asked himself, If I was Chatter, how would I be seeing all this? Seeing? Maybe that's it. I'll play the tugboat and she'll see what I want her to do.

He grabbed the loop and slid off the board. Taking the Velcro strap in his teeth, he began to swim. Billy noticed that the dolphin was showing interest. She moved closer to inspect this strange change in his behavior pattern.

He kicked on and muttered, "Tow . . . tow . . . tow . . ." again and again. After twenty repetitions, and a hundred yards more, he slowed to rest and reached to pet her. She hovered beside him, click-ticking, as if wanting to know more. Moving slowly, Billy took the leash from his mouth and slid the loop over Chatter's beak, all the while stroking her with his other hand. He could see she was about to cast it off and hurried to say the command: "Tow, Chatter. Tow!"

With an energetic beat of her powerful fluke, the dolphin surged ahead dragging the surfboard out of Billy's reach. He held back his scream of fear and spoke calmly, "That's great, Chatter. Bring it back, please."

She stopped some distance across the water and stared at him. Was she being mischievous, or did her behavior suggest a deeper meaning? Billy sensed that Chatter knew she held his life around her beak. He floated and watched her, waiting for the dolphin to make a decision. Billy sensed that yelling at Chatter would only drive her off. He tried to communicate the way he thought she might understand—by projecting his inner feelings to the dolphin. "Chatter, we're friends, and I need your help. Please tow the surfboard back to me. Come on, Chatter. I know you can understand what I'm sending out to you. Please bring the surfboard back."

With agonizing slowness the dolphin returned to him. He hugged her and climbed back on top of the surfboard thinking, Here's the test. I hope to God you understand, Chatter.

Aloud, Billy said with more confidence than he felt, "Okay, Chatter. Tow! Tow Billy!"

She turned to look at him and shook her head. The loop almost came off her beak and Billy thought, I'm being condescending, and she senses that.

He looked at her directly—one mammal in need of another. "Chatter. I'm wiped out. I need you to tow me. Now, please. Let's get going. Tow."

Her head went down, and with a strong beat of her fluke, the dolphin swam off so rapidly that Billy had to grasp the surfboard to keep from sliding off. As they sped across the water he realized that the dolphin was heading in the approximate direction of Samoa. *How in the hell did she know which way I wanted to go?*

The young man and the dolphin continued southwestward— Billy paddling when his strength permitted, and Chatter towing him more and more frequently. Sunburn now reddened every inch of Billy's exposed skin. Blisters erupted on the back of his legs. No rain had fallen to replenish the empty water jug, and Billy was becoming dangerously dehydrated.

At noon on the seventh day, he gave up attempting to paddle and collapsed on the surfboard. He was close to giving up and allowing the sea to take him. *Just to drift into some long sleep where there's lots of water and a little shade now and then.*

The dolphin looked at Billy and sensed his state of resignation. She knew that her kind often met death with a resigned stillness. That was normal, but he was not of her kind, and she swam to nudge him with her beak. She poked his side, but this time Billy did not move. She pushed against him even harder. He rolled off the surfboard into the water and came alive. She saw the surprise on his face and was glad. Chatter splashed him with her fluke and turned to push him back onto the surfboard. She thrust her beak through the leash loop and began towing him once more. He lifted his head and saw far-off clouds. They were white puffy ones that form over land. And not too far forward of the clouds, flocks of seabirds skittered over the surface diving for bait fish. Far off, the faint outline of a high gray-green island showed in the distance. "Look at that, Chatter! That's land! There's water there! And food, and shade, and everything! We did it! Just one more day!"

The dolphin heard his excited sounds and they gave her a warm glow of pleasure.

With renewed energy, Billy slipped the leash off her beak and began paddling slowly for the faraway island. At sundown he collapsed from exhaustion. Chatter swam to him and nuzzled his neck. He made sounds and rubbed her head. She liked his touch and understood he wanted to go to the island. She slipped her beak through the noose and swam on. Echolocating ahead, she detected the reef fronting the beach and the schools of fish swimming amid the coral. She was hungry, but that want would soon be satisfied.

He awoke to the sound of waves breaking and he opened his eyes to stare at the island. A hundred yards off he saw a long curving beach with several outrigger canoes sitting on the sand. Behind the shore was a small village of thatched palapas sitting under coconut palms. Still farther back, forested mountains thrust into the sky.

He stroked Chatter and said, "You must have towed me all night."

Billy began paddling slowly for the beach. Where the gentle swells turned into waves, he stopped to look at the village. People were staring in his direction. As he hesitated, unsure of what to do next, Chatter rubbed her beak against his leg. He looked down at the dolphin and knew she couldn't be with him anymore. He touched her lightly and said sadly, "I gotta go now, Chatter . . . to be with my kind."

He slid into the water and put his arms around the dolphin. Holding back tears, he climbed back on the board and murmured to her, "God, how I love you. Have a good life, Chatter."

He looked back, saw a small wave building, and paddled to catch it. As weak as he was, Billy couldn't resist a ride. He slid down the face of the little breaker and came slowly to his feet. He glanced back, looking for Chatter. All he saw was the dazzle of sea and sun that had punished him so mercilessly. The world spun. Little bright stars filled his mind, and he fell.

CHAPTER ELEVEN

Coconut oil rubbed gently into his sunburns, daily bathing in fresh water, and a diet rich in greens, fresh fish, and ripe fruit helped Billy to recover quickly. Even so, it was two days before he realized he was lying in a hammock under the shade of a palm frond hut. He opened his eyes to take in a small village facing a sparkling lagoon. Next he saw several children and an old white-haired man staring at him. The memory of his long, arduous paddle came back with a rush, and Billy asked, "How long have I been here?"

Children giggled and the old man said with a slight English accent, "Two days, young man. We're very glad, indeed, to see you looking so chipper. Now, rest. Later, tell us where you came from and we can sort out what to do with you."

"Where am I now?"

"Totua Island, Samoa, a day's sail east of Pago Pago." The

old man smiled and added, "And a world away from earthly cares, dear fellow."

"You're English?"

"Let us say I've had a British education. Now rest."

As Billy recovered, he watched the fishermen launch their pangas at dawn and return each noon with the catch. On the third day, Billy felt strong enough to walk to the shore and help them carry fish up to the communal trough where they were cleaned and divided among the villagers. His blistered skin was healing quickly, and he looked forward to paying his keep by going fishing with the men. As he struggled across the hot sand he stared beyond the gentle, spilling waves. The blueness stretched to eternity. After a long moment he turned from the water and realized he had been searching for Chatter. He hoped she had found a pod to join.

At the end of his first week on the island he pulled the small sketch pad out of his frayed, salt-encrusted getaway bag and he began drawing pictures of a dolphin. The island children encouraged him with laughs and shouts of delight. He found himself making fast outlines of Chatter leaping out of the water and realized he was thinking about her all the time. One of the little kids jabbed a finger on the drawing and then pointed toward the lagoon. Then they shouted in their singsong English, "Billy! Billy! Da same kind in the water. Come quick!"

The excited children pulled Billy to his feet and led him to the beach. He looked over their heads toward the lagoon and his heart pounded. It couldn't be Chatter. She was gone. It must be another dolphin. They gestured out beyond the little waves and he saw a dorsal fin slicing through the calm water. He whistled and called her name, as he had done so many times. He held his breath. Suddenly the dolphin surged out of the sea, her head turning in the direction of his voice. Billy ran for the lagoon shouting, "Chatter!"

He sprinted through the shallows, with the children racing behind. In chest-deep water she leaped again and swam for him. Then she was nuzzling against him, quivering with that wonderful life force that had helped Billy survive his long ordeal. He grabbed her fin and she began towing him toward shore. When they were among the excited children he let Chatter go and she swam among them. They shrieked in fear and ran for the beach. He called Chatter to him and began stroking her. The children stopped and watched the young man playing with the dolphin. He waved them closer and they cautiously eased up to her. Within minutes, Chatter's affectionate response to the children eased their fears. With Billy helping them, they soon were taking turns being towed about the shallows.

In the late afternoon, when the ocean breeze stilled and the sun's glare softened, Billy sat beside the water drawing quick sketches of Chatter, who floated only feet away. She seemed to like posing, or she was happy being with him again. After the paper was crowded with her likeness, Billy stood and waded out to show the dolphin his drawings. Chatter cocked her head and whistled approval. Billy thought with astonishment, She recognizes her image. I wonder if . . . ?

He began another drawing, a fast outline of *Lucky Dragon*. He placed the sketch before Chatter. Watching for her reaction he asked, "How do you like this one?"

The dolphin whistled her distress call. With a tremendous leap, she turned to race for deeper water. She dove and then surfaced to wag her head rapidly, expressing alarm. Billy called her back and she slowly approached him. *She recognized* Lucky Dragon*'s shape. That means she comprehends symbols, and we can understand each other by drawings. Could we really learn to communicate that way?*

As Chatter swam closer, he held up the drawing of the tuna clipper. Though still agitated, Chatter didn't flee. Instead, she lunged at the paper, ripping the sketch out of Billy's hands. With her beak, Chatter shoved the drawing of the clipper underwater, battering it back and forth until the sodden paper was shredded and drifted apart. He was dumbfounded and thought, You reminded me of a promise I'm going to keep. He bent down, put his face against Chatter's, and whispered to her, "Want to help me find *Lucky Dragon* and get that guy?"

Billy explained his vow to the white-haired elder, who said, "You have taken on a quest as difficult as the search for the Holy Grail. Where is it you want to go first?"

"Suva, Fiji, where I signed aboard. From there, I'm not sure how to get to Costa Rica, but I will."

"And your friend from the sea?"

Billy shook his head as if unable to plan that far ahead.

The elder explained, "Suva is easy. There's the mail schooner, but after that you must use your wits. And I tell you one thing, young man: not everything is as it seems."

"Don't I know it."

Two weeks later, the interisland schooner eased against the

Suva docks, and Billy looked about the harbor. The little West-sail that he had admired was still anchored off the seawall in front of the bench, where he had painted the sturdy sloop. And the For Sale notice still showed in the cabin window.

As the schooner brushed against the dock, Billy made sure Chatter was alongside. He called to her, and she poked her head up and whistled at him. He was amazed at her loyalty and endurance. She had cruised beside the mail schooner all the long sail to Fiji and seemed as energetic and curious as always.

He jumped off the boat and walked along the harbor wall with Chatter swimming after him. He wasn't worried about her. She often vanished for hours, only to return and take up her position forward of the schooner's bow, often surfing its wake. Billy called to the dolphin, "Hey, Chatter. If you get hungry, don't wait for me. I'm heading into the town for a real restaurant."

Billy walked on, following the seawall and froze in his tracks. Fifty yards ahead floated a small ship he had seen before. He remembered the twin dolphin logo on her bow and the Zodiacs lashed to the stern. It was the same vessel he had stared at from *Lucky Dragon*'s helicopter.

He broke into a fast walk. When he was alongside the gangplank, he looked up to the bridge. The young woman he had admired through the magnification of Arnold's bin-oculars was standing by the railing cleaning the lens of a video camera. She was even more lovely at close range and filled her T-shirt and tight shorts with graceful, muscled curves. Billy had been right. She was amazing, and he felt something more than physical. He continued to watch her until she sensed his interest and turned to glance down at him. Their eyes met and held for a long moment. She smiled faintly and asked, "Do I know you?"

Taking the initiative, Billy grinned at her and started up the gangplank. "We've seen each other before, and I'll bet you dinner tonight you can't guess where."

Billy won the bet. Dinner was at sunset, on *Salvador*'s aft deck. Billy, Sarah, Captain Seeger, and a few of the crew sat around a hatch-cover table under an early rising moon. When Benny Seeger learned that Billy had sailed aboard *Lucky Dragon*, he insisted the young man recount his ordeal.

Billy was finishing the story of his misadventures and sensed Captain Seeger's disbelief. He could see that Sarah was fascinated by his tale, and there was no doubt she accepted the truth of his words. Several of the other young crew members were nodding, but all were waiting for the captain's verdict.

Billy went on, ". . . so when I get my act together, and a boat, Chatter and I are going after him. I don't know exactly how we're going to pull it off, but we're going to stop what he's been doing!"

Sarah frowned, showing doubt for the first time. With a tone that suggested that Billy might be brain-damaged, she said, "You and that dolphin? You're dreaming."

He shrugged and grinned innocently. The captain leaned forward and spoke to her. "Don't you understand, Sarah? He knows how Gandara operates, where he fishes, and he's the only witness we have to his activities."

She faced Billy and asked, "About that cannery buyer,

could you identify him again, and the company name?"

"Sure. The guy was some yuppie wimp. And it's Universal Brands. Their tuna's in all the supermarkets. You know, Sea Fresh Tuna. And you gotta remember their stupid commercial with Tommy the dancing tuna. . . ."

He began singing the melody to the old jingle. "*Sea Fresh Tuna hits the spot. A lot of food value in the can we got. In salads and sandwiches you're going to love Sea Fresh!*"

Sarah appeared uneasy and spoke to Benny, bringing the conversation back to business. "We might have a case a judge would listen to, if we can prove Universal Brands is in violation of the Marine Mammal Protection Act."

"And it would be three years before a trial. And if we won, they'd only pay a slap-on-the-wrist fine. How many more dolphins are going to die between now and then? We've got to change our plan."

Seeger stared at the younger man as if making a decision about him and said, "I buy that you were aboard *Lucky Dragon*, but really, as much as I find dolphins incredible, it's hard to believe that you and . . ."

Billy stood and looked down at Seeger as if accepting his challenge. Without a word, he left the table and walked quickly to the stern. He gazed across the shimmering water as the others moved to join him at the railing. He thought, You'd better be there.

He put his thumb and index finger between his lips and whistled loudly, then called into the night, "Chatter!"

He held his breath. Nothing. Where was she? From across the harbor came her answering click-ticking. Moments later,

Chatter surfaced beside the ship and leaped out of the water. She surged upward as high as the railing. Before she fell back the dolphin seemed to hover and stare at them.

Billy felt his love go out to her. Sarah gave Billy a surprised look and said, "I've read about dolphins becoming attached to people, but in all the scientific literature—"

"Forget science. She saved my life."

Benny put an arm around Billy's shoulder and led him back to the table. Billy had a feeling he was being courted, but he let the captain do the talking. "You're going to need a place to bunk and eat. So how about moving aboard? And think about joining the crew."

He noticed that Sarah gave the captain a frown as if she didn't approve of the invitation. Seeger ignored her and prompted, "How about it, Billy? We have the same goals. Sail with us."

Billy took a bite of grilled steak. "You eat well on *Salvador*."

"This is dining. At sea, we eat and chase pirate tuna clippers. What do you say?"

He turned his attention to Sarah. He felt a romantic hunger rising and saw that she sensed his interest. She turned her eyes away, and Billy shifted his attention back to Seeger. "It's a tempting offer, but there's Chatter. At *Salvador*'s speed, she couldn't keep up all the way to Central America."

Getting back to business, Sarah asked, "How often does Gandara put into port to unload?"

"I couldn't say. He sold his catch once while I was aboard, to that American cannery in Samoa."

"So how would you get close to him?" asked the captain.

"In a small sailboat that Chatter could follow. Like that Westsail sloop anchored behind us. He wouldn't suspect that. With any luck I could get photos or video of him killing dolphins."

"You may be right. Every time we get close, he sends up his chopper and hauls ass."

Benny rushed on as if he were an admiral planning a sea battle. "So you find him with his net out, shoot videotape, and we'd be right over the horizon waiting for you to radio us."

"Then what?"

"When he's stopped dead in the water, we charge in and ram him!"

"Hey, I'm not in this to kill anyone. And besides, he'd recognize me."

"We'll disguise you. Grow a beard. Hell, he thinks you're dead."

Sarah leaned forward and said, "He could be fishing anywhere from Peru to Mexico. How would you find him?"

"Chatter could," Billy said with confidence.

Seeger lifted a hand to signal that he had heard enough and was about to make a decision. Offering a carrot of temptation, the captain asked, "Do you think that little sloop would do the job?"

Billy turned to look longingly at the moon-silvered outline of the Westsail.

They stood on the seawall inspecting the boat. The beamy, canoe-ended sloop showed the ravages of weathering, but to Billy's eyes she was a beautiful, seaworthy little vessel, and the floating embodiment of his dream. He turned to Benny and Sarah and said happily, "The Westsail's a class boat. I'll bet there are a couple hundred of them sailing around the world right now. They're proven blue-water cruisers, and that one's set up to sail single-handed."

Sarah regarded this intense young man who had so unexpectedly entered her life. He was bringing forth emotions in her she didn't want to feel. Still, she liked his boyish, enthusiastic grin. "Billy, it's so small—"

"Oh, hell, Sarah. Don't be a worrywart," Benny muttered. "That's the size boat we want. The elephant and the mouse. David and Goliath, remember? What do you think, Billy?"

"She'll do if the rigging and hull are sound," he said, trying to project a confidence he didn't really feel. He had sailed a lot off Southern California, but always within sight of land. The thought of an open ocean, of deep-water passages from Fiji to Central America, seemed beyond him. He glanced at the water where Chatter cruised back and forth and asked himself if he would be leading her on some fool's crusade.

Benny turned to Sarah and ordered, "Have her hauled out. If she passes a survey, we'll make an offer."

"Benny, our budget . . . We're running short of money already," Sarah protested.

The captain looked down at Chatter swimming alongside the seawall and said, "Talk to that dolphin about money. I'm sure she'll understand."

He started back along the seawall, then he paused and called back, "And you two are in charge of making that pea pod ready for sea."

The burly captain hurried off, and Billy sensed that he had been given more than the job of having the boat inspected. He guessed that Benny was testing him, and if he did well, then the boat was his. He wondered if winning the captain's respect would give him permission to get close to Sarah. Billy glanced at her and his stomach flip-flopped. He turned to Sarah and said, "Let's check the boatyards and find a marine surveyor."

"Uh, Billy? What exactly is a marine surveyor?"

"So, ah, boats and water stuff aren't your usual line of work, right?"

"Hardly," she said feeling put down. "I make videos—you know, documentary stuff."

As they walked along the seawall for the inner harbor, Billy asked, "How come you're hunting guys like Gandara with Benny Seeger?"

She began to talk about herself and her movie producer father, revealing more than she had ever intended. "My dad really knows how to make movies. He had me shooting Super 8 film when I was ten. Like some kids are forced to play Little League, my father insisted I learn to shoot and edit film, add a soundtrack, titles, and credits. When he'd project my films to his movie biz friends I used to feel sick. He wanted me to be a camera operator, to have a trade. And later on a director. So, here I am on *Salvador* with a film crew ready to tape a pirate tuna clipper killing dolphins that Benny can't chase down."

Billy asked, "How come you haven't mentioned your mom?"

She took a breath, decided not to reveal the hurt and said, "She split from my father. It was a messy divorce. She's independently wealthy for life now and lives in London."

"Sort of what happened to my folks, except my dad's dead and I don't know where my mother is these days."

With a surge of compassion Sarah reached out to Billy and hugged him. Despite her surprise at being so open, she found being with this innocent young man, with his wide surfer's shoulders and peeling nose, refreshingly easy. *And he doesn't want to use me to get close to my father.*

Billy wanted to know more about her. "Why aren't you working in the movie business now?"

"After finishing high school, I couldn't decide if I should go to college, work as a camera operator, or find a job in some sort of environmental organization."

"Like what's environmental?"

"Sierra Club, Greenpeace, National Wildlife Federation, Sea Shepherd. So I went to work with my father raising money to send Benny out here."

"He's a radical guy."

"He's doing things that need to be done. And here I am."

They walked on, talking about dolphins. It was safe talk, and she told him about swimming with Benny and being among the dolphins in the wild for the first time. "It was mind-blowing. After that, I really understood what Benny was trying to do."

Billy glanced at Chatter and then found the nerve to ask Sarah what he desperately wanted to know. "You and Benny, are you two, ah . . . ?"

"Together? Lord, no. He's more than I could handle."

With a grin, Billy said, "That clears the air."

She gave him an inquiring glance, but his attention had

shifted to the entrance of a large boatyard. By the office door a sign announced, CHRIS CRABB—MARINE SURVEYOR.

Later that afternoon, while Billy was having the Westsail hauled out for inspection, Sarah watched Benny load a digital videotape into a small Sony camcorder. He handed her the camera and said, "You might as well start teaching Billy how to shoot this. If he can get good stuff, we'll get on the networks. And maybe I can sell some of it."

"Hey, Benny. Fund-raising is my job, remember?"

"Okay. When you get back, raise enough for a chopper."

"When are we going home?"

"If that kid can get the goods, and after I sink Gandara, we'll head back."

She looked through the viewfinder and framed it on Benny's weathered face. Hesitantly, she said, "I'm not sure I want to be responsible for sending Billy after *Lucky Dragon*."

"Nobody's forcing him."

"He almost got himself killed once."

"If you have any doubts, you should have stayed home and played with the dolphins at SeaWorld."

"They're doing important research there, Benny."

"Theoretical bullshit. Out here, the dolphins are free to do what they do."

She resisted the urge to argue with him and said simply, "Tell me, Benny. What do dolphins do out here?"

His serious frown changed abruptly to a mischievous grin that told Sarah he was making peace with her. With utter sincerity, Benny said softly, "They do no harm. . . ."

CHAPTER TWELVE

The sloop came down the ways and slid into the water with a massive splash. Billy stood in the Westsail's cockpit holding a shroud to keep from falling overboard and yelled at Sarah, "All right! All right!"

She had refused to ride the boat into the harbor and remained on the dock looking at the freshly painted Westsail with its polished brass reflecting the harsh tropic sun. Chatter cruised beside the sloop and Billy reached out to pet her. Feeling left out, Sarah murmured to herself, "Boys and their toys."

She glanced at the small waterproof aluminum camcorder case she held. "And I've got another toy for him."

He started the engine. The little gasoline-powered Atomic Four sputtered to life. Billy put the boat alongside the seawall and helped her aboard. They motored on toward *Salvador* and Sarah remarked, "She seems seaworthy now. What's next?"

"Next, we have to name her," he said with a grin, as if he had a surprise waiting. "Got any ideas?"

"Since you're the captain, what name would you like?"

"The *Sarah*."

She felt herself blushing and impulsively reached out to hug him.

He moored the sloop behind the old minesweeper and she watched him drop the boat's small inflatable dinghy over the side and tie it to the stern. She had no idea what he was doing. To cover her uncertainty about things nautical she went into the small, neat cabin to make coffee. Here was familiar territory. She had helped him paint the interior a bright, light-reflecting white, and had arranged to have the mattresses of the two narrow bunks recovered with new, bright orange cotton canvas. Sarah was surprised that such a confined space could be so functionally comfortable. Aft of the bunks, there was a small galley, and across from the stove, sink, and icebox were two padded benches with a table in between that sat four. The booth, Billy explained, also served as a flat surface to spread charts across.

Sarah ignited the propane gas stove and put a kettle on the burner. She had bought a small plastic filter cone, two hundred paper filters, and ten one-pound cans of coffee for the galley. No instant coffee for Billy. The cost of imported goods in Fiji was exorbitant, but she wanted Billy to have the best obtainable in Suva. She felt so guilty about spending the expedition's funds, she had paid for the coffee with her own money. Sarah poured almost-boiling water through the grounds that dripped into two heavy mugs. I don't even know how he likes it, she thought.

She stepped out of the cabin to ask him and peered over the stern. Billy had carefully painted the boat's new name—her name—on the transom in flowing script, and was now drawing a pair of spouting dolphins to grace each end of the lettering. She was flattered and asked, "Do you want sugar or canned milk in your coffee?"

"I hate canned milk, and no to the sugar. Black'll be fine."

He gestured at his work with the brush. "What do you think?"

"You are an artist."

"Some artist. The only painting I ever sold was of this boat."

She ducked into the cabin and brought out the coffee and a tray of fresh scones from a Suva bakery. He climbed aboard, took the mug she offered, and they sat down in the cockpit. She watched him take a bite of scone and smile with appreciation. She smiled back, feeling at ease with him now. Without speaking, they moved closer and she allowed herself to lean against him.

Without warning, Chatter surged out of the water and hovered over them for an instant. Billy reached out to pet her. With his attention on Chatter, he spoke slowly, as if having trouble expressing his thoughts. "Killing all those dolphins to catch tuna. That really got to me. And I thought there were laws to protect them."

"Those laws only apply to U.S.–owned boats. When American skippers used to fish down here they learned how to get them out of the nets, and they saved almost all of them."

"They used to?"

"It's difficult to guarantee dolphin-free tuna. So rather than risk potential fines and government hassle, they're fishing in the central Pacific where dolphins don't travel with tuna."

"What about the embargo?"

"Some of the tuna packers are lobbying to do away with it. Captains like Gandara fish without restrictions, and sell to companies getting around the embargo. You saw him unloading at that cannery in Samoa. We can't let it start again, Billy. And it won't if people understand and refuse to buy tuna caught with dolphins."

"Hell, people like their tuna salads and sandwiches. How do you reach them?"

She stood and entered the cabin. A moment later she returned and handed him the camcorder case. He opened it, lifted out the little Sony digital video camera and looked up at Sarah.

"You reach them, Billy, with gut-churning pictures of what it takes to put tuna in a can. You show bloody images of all those dolphins dying. And you film someone like Gandara killing them. Then you take that someone to court."

He lifted a hand to slow her down and said, "Hold on. You're sounding like a movie producer."

"Yeah, my father taught me how to grab an audience."

"And you need an airhead surfer like me to sail up to the net close enough to tape the slaughter before Benny rams 'em. Is that the game plan?"

"They won't know it's you."

"What is this? Some sort of enviro–CIA operation?"

"It's not about getting a tan and going surfing, Billy. And you said you wanted to get that guy."

"I'm all for sinking him. But I'm not a crusader. That's your game."

"Billy, it's not a game," she said imploringly.

He turned away to look at the water. Chatter sensed his glance and swam closer to be petted. She clicked at him and lifted her head for his touch. For a long moment he looked at her, remembering the long ordeal they had shared.

He returned his attention to Sarah. She was so appealing, so unlike any girl he had ever known. And yet, he wasn't sure he trusted her. Unable to keep his feelings hidden, he said, "And you and Benny have it planned so I'm to be the sacrificial lamb."

She sipped coffee and said lightly, "I'd say you were more of a Billy goat."

His somber mood changed abruptly. "Okay, you've got your goat. Chatter's getting hungry, and there are no fish in the harbor, so let's take her for a sail."

Outside the harbor a brisk wind filled the sloop's mainsail. The heavy keel kept the Westsail from heeling excessively, and her bow sliced through the choppy swells at a serene, comfortable speed. She was a joy to sail. Billy tested the self-steering vane and autopilot. Both worked properly. He could safely take short naps while the boat maintained a heading without him at the helm. He turned the wheel over to Sarah and went forward to raise the jib. He didn't like the idea of standing on the foredeck in a blow taking down the battering, flapping sailcloth with no one at the helm. *Maybe I shouldn't be sailing alone.*

Holding the forestay, he looked down at Chatter, who had taken up a position in the bow wake. He yelled at the dolphin. "What do you think of the boat?"

She heard his voice, lunged out of the water, and raced ahead to leap and spin before falling back into the sea.

"Yeah, I like her, too," he called out. Then Billy thought, But if I ever go over the side, and she sails on without me, I'm gone.

He turned to glance at Sarah, liking the way she stood relaxed and sure-footed gripping the wheel with the breeze ruffling her hair. He glanced back at the boat's wake. The trail of bubbling white foam was straight. She was steering well. He joined her in the cockpit and said, "You're doing great."

"Benny taught me how."

He pointed to an opening in the reef and said, "Let me show you how to bring her about. Then we'll sail into the lagoon and snorkel for lobster."

"I didn't bring a bathing suit."

"Some woman of the world you are," he teased.

He was surprised she was so bashful. She wouldn't go into the water until he had swum some distance away. Then she overcame her shyness, went down the boarding ladder with her back to him, and they swam together over the shallow lagoon. She followed behind as they flippered along, peering downward through diving masks, searching the coral forest for the waving feelers of spiny lobsters. He saw a likely-looking outcropping that might shelter one, drew in a lungful of air, and dove.

He looked under the coral. Far back in a narrow cave a pair

of long tapered feelers twitched. The creature sensed him and backed into the recess beyond his reach. Billy was desperately hungry for air and he swam for the surface watching the outline of Sarah's trim body framed by skylight from above. He laughed to himself and thought, I'm an underwater voyeur.

He burst into sunlight beside Sarah, startling her, and sucked in air to dive again. This time he spotted a lobster hiding in a crevice; it had no place to retreat. He shot his hand out and grabbed the top of its shell, the one area where its sharp spines wouldn't puncture his skin. It was too small to keep, but he surfaced to show off his catch. He thrust it at her, teasing, testing her. She reached out and touched its antenna gingerly. Her hand went over its back and Billy released the lobster. They floated closer, studying the little crustacean. She turned it over to glance at its underside. The lobster suddenly flicked its powerful tail and shot from her hands. Before it had gone a yard, Chatter raced between them and crunched the spiny creature in her powerful jaws. They watched her quickly grind the lobster into a pulp of shell and flesh and swallow it in one gulp.

Billy looked at Sarah. Her eyes were wide. She spit out the snorkel and said with wonder, "Did you see that? Your Chatter really showed a vicious streak."

"She's hungry. What did you expect, love and kisses? And *we* put 'em in pots of boiling water, alive."

He dove again, found another lobster, and tossed it into the sloop, saying, "One more, and we can have dinner."

In shallower water where they could stand, he spotted another pair of antennae protruding out of a coral head. He led Sarah down, showed her the feelers, and pantomimed how she should grab the lobster. She reached for it, but the spiny creature shot out from the coral. Billy kicked after it and his flippers knocked off Sarah's mask. He dove to retrieve her face-plate. At the same moment Sarah ducked under to grab the mask and they came into each other's arms. Then Chatter's hard beak thrust between them. With a toss of her head, the dolphin forced the couple apart and leaped out of the water with a burst of click-ticks as if scolding them.

Frightened from the surprise interruption, she shouted at Billy, "What is it between you two? Is she jealous?"

"She's kind of possessive. I guess it's because we've been through a lot together."

When they were back aboard and toweling themselves dry, Sarah remarked, "I've read accounts of dolphins becoming romantically attracted to humans. . . ."

"Look, all I know is that she saved my life, and I guess I saved hers. So let it go at that."

Billy turned from her and walked to the bow to haul the anchor. On the deck the one lobster he had caught lay baking in the sun. As he picked it up, the animal flapped its spiked tail in protest. Seeing that Chatter was out of sight, he carefully released it into the sea.

Two days later Billy dropped into the cabin and returned to memorizing where each line, sail, and spare part was stored. There was a vast assortment of food, gear, and tools. In an emergency, and especially in the night, he would have to know where to find what he needed quickly. Benny had okayed every item on his shopping list, but Sarah questioned the need of the new

Korean Goldstar twenty-nautical-mile-range radar that cost almost five thousand dollars installed and calibrated.

In every locker there were tins of corned beef, Spam, sardines, soups, stews, pineapple chunks, peach slices, jam, peanut butter, boxes of fast-cooking noodles, instant cereals, rice, soda crackers, bottles of sauces, fruit juices, dried fruit, granola bars, cookies, and a fifty-pound stalk of green bananas. There were two dozen coconuts, four mangos, and six papayas for the first few days at sea. Oranges and lemons would keep longer. In little cubbyholes he found assorted treats that Sarah had bought on impulse in Suva's one supermarket. He muttered, "It's like I was sailing around the world with a crew. I hope I won't be at sea that long."

He marveled at Sarah's organizational ability. She had compiled the shopping list, noted where the supplies would be stored, and carefully stowed each item in every locker, shelf, and cabinet aboard. The little head forward of the vee-berths was so jammed with containers that there was hardly room to use the toilet. Billy thought, I might sink in a storm, but for sure I won't starve to death.

He saw Sarah and Benny arriving. She was carrying a long rectangular carton wrapped in brown paper. He wondered what it was. Then Benny spoke to him and he forgot to ask.

"Billy, I just got an e-mail from Air New Zealand that the generator parts are coming in tomorrow. If they're the right ones, we'll pull out of here in a week, and probably be off Costa Rica a couple weeks before you arrive."

He closed the engine cover and stood to face Captain Seeger. Benny put a hand on his shoulder, squeezed it gently, and added, "If I don't get a chance to see you in the morning before you sail, thanks, and good luck. And never doubt we'll back you up all the way."

"If I find Gandara, and if you get a chance to ram *Lucky Dragon*, aim for the stern. The crew sleeps forward."

"I understand."

"I want a promise, Benny."

"I'll do what I can."

"That's not good enough, Benny."

"Okay, you have my word. See you, Billy."

He walked off down the dock, shoulders square, as if he were on the bridge of *Salvador*. Billy thought, Hell of a guy, and a guy you could die or kill for. I hope to God it won't come to that.

He turned to look for Sarah. She was sitting in the cockpit holding a chilled orange soda for him. Beside her was the long package wrapped in brown paper.

He took the soda and she shoved the package at him. "A present from Benny. Go ahead. Open it."

He felt that Christmas-morning excitement. Could it be a fishing rod, or maybe a baseball bat? He peeled back the wrapper and saw the red-and-black Winchester Repeating Arms logo printed on the top of the brown cardboard box. "What's this all about?"

He worked the top off the carton and inside lay a gleaming lever-action .30-30 rifle and two boxes of cartridges. He lifted the rifle out of the box and sighted on a seagull sitting on the harbor railing. His father had taught him to shoot a .22 rifle long ago and the Winchester felt familiar in his hands. He levered the breech open and checked to make sure the rifle was unloaded. The chamber and magazine were empty. He turned to Sarah. "Hey, thanks. But, how come a rifle?"

"Benny thought you might need to protect yourself," she said evenly.

"A gun on a boat. Well, uh, I might get depressed from too many granola bars and kill myself, and if I ever had to shoot at anyone, they're gonna have guns too and shoot back."

He sensed she was hurt by his rejection, but Sarah covered her feelings with a smile and said, "Billy, please take it along. And stow it where you can reach it quickly."

"Sarah, you're hustling me. It's like I'm some ancient Greek warrior going off to battle . . . but I'm not slaying a bunch of Trojans for you or anyone else."

She moved closer to Billy and looked into his eyes. "Billy, it's not for me. You're doing this for Chatter, and all the other dolphins, remember?"

He let that sink in. Yeah, for Chatter, he thought and looked across the harbor for her. As if the dolphin sensed his thought, she surfaced and swam alongside the sailboat, click-ticking at him. Her nearness brought his boyish grin back. He turned to Sarah and said lightly, "Okay, I accept the rifle, and thanks. Have dinner with me on the boat. It'll be my last night ashore. . . ."

"I'll bring the food. I'm an excellent cook," she said happily.

Candles set on the engine cover glowed romantically in the sloop's cockpit and cast their soft glow on Billy and Sarah. She really *was* an excellent cook, Billy thought as he took another bite of the grilled ahi she had cooked on the boat's tiny hibachi. He complimented her, and Sarah said, "It's fresh from the fish market."

He wanted to tell her that the fish steaks labeled as Hawaiian ahi were often filleted from yellowfin tuna caught with dolphins. Instead, he said, "I'm going to miss you, Sarah . . . especially on those long, lonely night watches."

He slid closer to her and she leaned against him. For a long moment they looked toward the night sky and the Southern Cross twinkling overhead. As if her thought had come from far away, she asked softly, "What time are you leaving in the morning?"

"Right after the market opens. I want to take on a few more fresh goodies, and put a chunk of ice in the box."

She turned to rest her head against his shoulder. He moved to kiss her, but they were interrupted by Chatter's squawking coming from alongside the hull. Billy pulled away from Sarah and leaned over the railing. "Not now. Get out of here. Go catch a fish or something!"

He turned to Sarah and said, "It's getting chilly. Want to go into the cabin?"

"It's lovely out here . . . and your friend seems to want to keep an eye on you."

He looked over the side again, gave the dolphin an annoyed glance, and turned back to Sarah. "I think I'm falling in love with you."

"When you're really sure about that, let me know."

She stood and began clearing away the dishes. He moved to help and said, "I'm sure."

"Who's going to break the news to the other woman?"

He stood on the rail and looked down at Chatter. "Hey, Chatter. This is going to come as a surprise. I love you a whole bunch, but there's someone else. . . ."

Still feeling a sense of fun, Billy turned back to Sarah. She was standing on the dock staring at him and looking serious. "Good night, Billy. Be very careful out there."

She turned and walked off. Billy watched her vanish into the darkness and shook his head in bewilderment. Whatever he had done to displease her was a mystery to him. He turned to look for Chatter. The dolphin eased silently out of the water. He stroked her head and thought, What was that all about . . . ?

CHAPTER THIRTEEN

The cultured accent of the British Broadcasting Corporation's nightly news announcer set Benny's teeth on edge. He much preferred the rapid, self-assured style of CNN's reporters, but that news program didn't provide the international coverage he was listening for. He had been pacing *Salvador's* dark bridge, waiting to hear the results of the latest international trade agreements and learn how the U.S. Congress would respond. The countries that had signed the General Agreement on Tariffs and Trade were meeting in New York. One of the subjects on their agenda involved lifting the embargo that the United States had placed on tuna caught with dolphins. Benny was hoping the BBC's economic reporter would include news from the GATT meeting, and his expectation was fulfilled.

Over the shortwave radio's loudspeaker came the BBC report, "In a recent decision against the Americans, the GATT panel ruled that the United States had violated international trade agreements when it banned tuna imports because the fish were caught using methods that kill dolphins. In Washington, the U.S. Congress has directed the American president, through the U.S. trade representative, to renegotiate the treaty to recognize domestic environmental laws—"

Benny swore, "Why in the hell doesn't the president take a stand? The Mexicans and the others are going to get their tuna into the country again, and there goes another half a million dolphins!"

He turned his attention back to the BBC as the reporter added, "The United States, under pressure from environmental groups, will require a certificate of origin for all tuna caught in large drift nets in the South Pacific. This is yet another example of the conflict between U.S. environmental laws and international trade agreements.

"It appears that the U.S. is tightening its restriction against the use of high-seas drift nets by Japan, Korea, and Taiwan, while at the same time relaxing its embargo against Mexican-caught netted tuna. The rationale behind this policy inconsistency appears to be the administration's push for an expansion of a Latin America/U.S. free trade bill—"

He wanted to discuss the implications of the news with Sarah and left the bridge to find her. He knocked on her cabin door. There was no response. Benny turned the handle and looked inside. Her bunk was empty.

Far to the east, Louis Gandara stood on the bridge of his clipper enjoying the night and *Lucky Dragon*'s steady progress toward Costa Rica. He was remembering long-ago days in Africa until he was distracted by BBC's nightly news transmission. The distant signal was amplified and sent to the bridge speaker. He had been waiting anxiously for the news. With the report that the GATT panel held the United States in violation of trade agreements, Louis Gandara smiled knowingly. *I think I'll register* Lucky Dragon *in Mexico. With a few more years of good fishing, perhaps I'll return to Mozambique. Perhaps the new government has forgotten, and if not, perhaps they can be induced to forget, if my contributions are sufficiently well-placed.*

He missed Southern Africa, and the power his family once held. The Gandara estates had been vast, measured in hundreds of square kilometers. He remembered riding his horse along the deserted beaches facing the Indian Ocean. He recalled galloping for miles on the hard-packed, sparkling white sands and never seeing a footprint. With a frown he thought, I wonder if there are hotels there now.

His musings were interrupted by the bridge radio watch. The seaman reported, "There's a message for you on the company frequency, captain."

Gandara nodded and thought, They've been listening to BBC as well. He stepped onto the bridge and glanced at the radar scope. Except for sea clutter and low clouds to the east, the screen was empty of returns. That was a blessing. He would sleep well tonight and dream of Africa.

What *Lucky Dragon*'s radar and sonar didn't reveal was a pod of nearby dolphins heading in the same easterly direction. The pod's new leader sent out a burst of echolocating sound from his bulbous forehead. An instant later he detected the familiar metallic shape of the clipper. He had learned and began veering away from the threatening object. The dolphins, and the tuna accompanying them, were ravenous, but soon they would feed. The leader's keen senses had picked up a faint decrease in salinity levels that told him the pod was approaching a landmass where freshwater rivers flowed into the sea. His biological memory was guiding him on as surely as *Lucky Dragon* followed the electronic navigation signals broadcast from satellites orbiting under the same Southern Cross, far, far overhead.

CHAPTER FOURTEEN

The stalk of green bananas hanging from the sloop's mast had started to ripen, and Billy began counting them. There were seventy-two in all. Billy noticed that the ones at the top of the stalk were showing a hint of yellow. The first would soften and be ready to eat in about a week. *After that . . . It's bananas three times a day. Maybe I can dry some, or make banana bread.*

Billy had discovered that after the first hours of sailing alone his tension eased, and he let the sloop have her head. By day's end, he would be out of sight of land. He glanced back for a last reassuring look at the gray-green forested hills of Fiji already receding into the distance. He wondered if he would ever see trees again.

He looked at the white wake spilling off the bow. Chatter was there like she was chained to the boat. Billy realized that the dolphin hadn't left her position since they sailed out of Suva Harbor. He thought about that. Chatter usually foraged widely, but today she wouldn't leave the boat. That troubled him. He knew that whenever she changed her behavior pattern it was for a reason. "What's she trying to tell me? Maybe I'd better take a look forward."

He engaged the autopilot. Before moving to the bow he connected a line from his safety harness to the stainless steel cable railing. He knew that this procedure must become habit, and that no matter how tired or sleepy he was, his life depended on his connection to the boat.

Billy stood on the bow holding the forestay and stared at Chatter. She glanced up at him, and then with a loud click-ticking, pointed her beak at the bow. He called down to her, "I know that look. What's going on, Chatter?"

When the dolphin repeated her signal Billy began an inch-by-inch inspection of the bow area. He couldn't find anything amiss and sat on the anchor locker hatch trying to puzzle out the dolphin's odd behavior. On impulse, Billy pulled the hatch cover off and peered inside. With utter amazement he swore, "What the hell are you doing in there?"

Sarah stood and grinned at him. Her white sweatshirt and jeans were streaked with rust from the anchor chain, and her skin had that yellowish pallor that suggested seasickness wasn't far away.

She reached out for him and said, "Don't be angry, Billy. I couldn't let you go after *Lucky Dragon* alone."

He took her wrist, and none too gently hauled her out of the cramped anchor locker. Fighting back his anger, he turned and retreated to the cockpit. Then he shouted at her. "What do you think this is? Some kind of Beverly Hills fund-raiser for sweet little dolphins?"

He shoved the tiller hard to come about, and she demanded, "What are you doing?"

"Taking you back to Suva."

"Billy, you can't steer, watch the radar, listen to the radio, shorten sail, cook your meals, navigate, and stay alert twenty-four hours a day for the next five weeks!"

"You have no idea what you're getting into. Gandara's a killer—"

"If you get sick or hurt out here, who's going to sail the boat?" Sarah glanced over the side and added, "Certainly not your friend Chatter."

"There'll be storms, you'll get seasick, and there's only enough food for one," he shot back.

"Says you. I stowed provisions for both of us, with two weeks extra, in case we're becalmed. Yes, I was planning to be with you all along. And I can cook."

"So you said . . ."

"And I've been doing a lot of reading about boats and seamanship, and I can steer."

"Yeah, a boat with an engine. Under sail, you can't always point in the direction you want to go. We're heading east-northeast, but the wind's coming from that direction, so you tack back and forth, keeping track of how long one way, how long the other."

Billy saw she looked bewildered. "Okay, we'll start with the basics. And that's an old sailor's saying . . . one hand for yourself and one for the ship. Then it's knot tying and . . ."

She looked around the deck, spotted a length of braided rope used to secure the tiller, and snatched it up. With a grin, she put the line behind her and shut her eyes, then said teasingly, "Bet you can't tie a bowline behind your back with your eyes closed."

He couldn't ignore her challenge and snapped back, "Bet you I can!"

A moment later Sarah opened her eyes and handed him the line, now tied in a loop with a perfect bowline.

He took the rope and she could see he was impressed. She watched him untie the knot and place the line behind him. "You have to shut your eyes, remember?"

"Oh, for Christ's sake," he muttered, closing his eyes. She watched him struggling with the rope. A minute passed and Billy's face grew red. She knew she had him. Then he relaxed and handed her the limp strand of nylon that dangled untied like overcooked spaghetti. With a shrug, followed by his innocent grin, he said, "Welcome aboard."

"Thank you, Billy."

"But you have to remember, there's only one captain, and that's me. And there will be times when I tell you to do something without an explanation, and you have to do it, no questions asked. Do you get that one hundred percent?"

"I understand clearly, Billy," she answered, remembering Benny Seeger saying almost the same words.

"Now the first rule on this boat is . . . under sail, you never move out of the cockpit without hooking your safety line to the cable."

"Even when it's calm, like now?"

"Do you want to go back to Fiji?"

Ten days later the bananas all ripened at once. They had eaten as much of the yellow-and-black-spotted fruit as they could, Billy more than he should have. He was feeling the effect of the sloop's constant pounding into a choppy bow-on swell, but wouldn't admit he was actually seasick.

She sat down beside him and began slowly peeling the skin back from her fifth banana of the day. The fruit was already dark and fermenting. He watched Sarah gulp down a big bite. At that moment his stomach revolted. He mumbled for her to take the tiller and leaned over the stern. He forced himself to stare at the undulating horizon, but that did no good. A moment later he threw up. When his retching stopped, Billy saw that Chatter was swimming nearby and watching him. He forced a weak smile and said, "I'll be okay."

The dolphin swam closer, and Sarah saw Billy reach out to stroke Chatter's head. With a slight quiver she came halfway out of the sea to quickly nuzzle her beak against Billy's cheek. The dolphin's fluid movement, and seeming compassion, disturbed Sarah. *It's like they're mates, or something. What's really going on between them?*

By noon the next day the seas had calmed and the surface lay smooth and oily. The wind that had helped them east-ward some two hundred nautical miles a day had died, and the *Sarah* ghosted along under limp sails, barely making two knots. The sun beat down with a relentless harshness, reflected off the ocean's mirrorlike cap, burning their bodies and eyes.

Billy warned that ultraviolet blindness was a real possibility and nagged Sarah to wear her sunglasses. By three o'clock the remaining bananas were black and almost flowing out of their skins. They tossed them overboard, and Billy gave the okay to walk around the boat without hooking up a safety line.

Sarah watched him restlessly prowl the boat inspecting fittings, adjusting shrouds, peering into the engine compartment—checking, always checking. Since he had discovered her in the anchor locker, Billy had been friendly enough, but there was no sense of intimacy. Sarah wondered if he had hidden resentments or anger, or was his attachment to the dolphin stronger than her appeal? She observed that for the last twenty minutes his attention had shifted from the boat to the water, and his focus was on Chatter. She wanted to ask what was holding his interest, but she knew a question would annoy him. Billy tired easily of her questions, and once, when his patience wore thin he snapped at her, "If you'd just look and think a while before asking, you'd find the answer right in front of your nose."

She did observe that Chatter kept surfacing off the bow to look at Billy, and for no apparent reason would turn away and swim off on a heading some degrees from their course. The dolphin repeated her pattern again and again until Billy announced, "She wants me to head in that direction, but why?"

Billy slung binoculars around his neck and climbed the mast with swift, strong agility. He stood on the crosstree and peered in the direction the dolphin seemed to want them to take.

Sarah needed to know what was going on, to have things explained, and called up to Billy, "Chatter's trying to tell us something, isn't she?"

"Yeah, but I can't figure out what. If only we could really talk!"

He slid down a stay and dropped into the cabin beside her. Sarah said, "She probably senses other dolphins, or—"

"Or *Lucky Dragon*!"

"Oh, come on, Billy. We're a long way from Central America. She's bewitched you."

"Well, maybe she's picking up the stink of his garbage, or hearing something from a pod he's setting a net on right this minute. Like distress calls or something."

"Billy, she's a remarkable animal, but—"

"Let me show you just how smart she really is . . ."

He dashed into the cabin and came back holding his sketch pad. She watched him draw a symbolic outline of a tuna clipper. When he was satisfied with his sketch, he whistled Chatter back to the sloop and showed her the drawing. To Sarah's amazement, the dolphin emitted a series of agitated clicks and whistles that she now recognized as alarm signals. Abruptly, Chatter raced off on the same heading she had been taking for the past hour.

Billy faced Sarah and insisted, "She's trying to tell me what course to follow to find *Lucky Dragon*, and we're going that way."

"If you say so," Sarah replied softly, not wanting to anger him. "I suppose there's only one way to find out."

"Chatter says so," he answered with conviction and pulled the tiller to put the sloop on the heading that Chatter had again taken. She saw the dolphin rise out of the sea and glance at them. Could she understand their conversation?

When the sloop was clearly on the new course, Chatter

swam back to the boat and took her usual position off the bow. Sarah felt her annoyance rising. She glanced at Billy, who gave her a self-satisfied grin.

The wind freshened, and they sailed on. Billy raised the jib, and the Westsail's speed increased another knot and a half. She observed that the closer they came to the Central American coastline, the more withdrawn Billy became.

Three days later an orange-red sun climbed out of the eastern sky and the wind died altogether. Without a breeze, the heat beat down relentlessly, frying their brains and creating an oppressive, blinding aura around the boat. She wanted to ask Billy how long they would float here becalmed, but hesitated, thinking he would regard it as another of her unnecessary questions. She needed to talk with him, about him, about herself, about life and deep-down secrets that she had revealed to no one. *Wasn't this the time and place? Being out here, absolutely away from everything and everyone, without the slightest chance of interruption, should lead to us really getting a relationship going. I'll ask him anyway.*

"How long do you think we'll be becalmed?"

"Days, weeks, ten minutes. How would I know? I'm not a captain like Benny. If I had a weather fax satellite receiver, we'd have the big picture. But, hey, your guess is as good as mine."

He said the last with such resignation that her heart went out to him. She wanted to brighten the mood and asked, "Would it be safe to jump in and swim by the boat? We could play with Chatter."

His grin came back. He said happily, "Grab your mask and

snorkel. We'll dive in, scrub the algae from the bottom, and cool off. Last one in cooks tonight!"

Holding his mask, snorkel, and fins, Billy threw a scrub brush overboard and dropped into the water a moment before she emerged from the cabin.

She stood on the deck watching his bare white bottom and called, "That's not fair. I had to put on a bathing suit."

"You had to?"

She dropped into the water and followed Billy as he swam along the hull scrubbing the fiberglass. Chatter immediately joined them and seemed curious at his interest in the hull. Billy kicked a few yards away from the boat and floated with Sarah until Chatter shoved between them. Sarah watched Billy grab the dolphin's fin and descend with her. As they sank into the blue-gray depths, Sarah remembered snorkeling with Benny beside *Salvador*, and her first encounter with wild dolphins.

She watched them diving deeper and deeper, twisting and turning together in an animal-human ballet amid dancing shafts of light and bubbles, until Billy was forced to let go. He kicked frantically for the surface and popped up beside her. Gasping in air he shouted happily, "In my second life, I'm going to be a dolphin."

Chatter buzzed by them, turned abruptly, and came to a sudden stop before Billy. At the same moment came the familiar drumming bursts of echolocating ticks, chirps, and whistles. Sarah recalled the familiar dolphin sounds and fondly welcomed their arrival.

Billy looked wildly about and she saw his eyes grow wide with astonishment. Sarah called to him, "Dolphins."

Then they heard Chatter's rapid pinging. In a state of agitated excitement the dolphin leaped out of the water, spun, and fell back in beside them. An instant later, flashes of gray came racing for them. Suddenly, the dolphins were all around and Billy and Sarah were bombarded by an intense barrage of clicks, ticks, and whistles, intermingled with the beating of a hundred and more flukes. They whirled and dove, leaped and thrashed, until the sea became a seething explosion of foam. Some brushed against Billy and Sarah, one butted him roughly, another knocked her mask aside. Just as quickly, the pod vanished. Billy spun to search the sea. Once, twice, he twisted in a circle looking through the water. With a cry of anguish he called to Sarah. "Chatter went with them!"

"Billy, be glad that they found her. She's with her own kind now."

A soft breeze began, and they sailed slowly eastward. The searing heat and relentless sun beat down oppressively, adding to Billy's dejected mood. He had been silent for the past three hours, holding binoculars and looking for Chatter. Sarah knew his loss was real, but didn't try to comfort him. She felt rejected, and moved as far from Billy as she could. But she also felt compassion and remembered that the dolphin had been compassionate when Billy was seasick. Sarah stood and stepped into the cabin. Ten minutes later she set a tray in front of Billy: pineapple chunks, slices of tinned ham, crackers—his favorite lunch. She watched him reach for a slice of ham and wrap it around the pineapple. He was healing quickly, and she smiled inwardly. Gently, she placed her hands on his sunburned shoulders and said, "I'm truly sorry she went away, but it might be for the best."

"I guess you're right. I hope she has a good life and stays out of the nets." He looked up at her and added, "She's so smart, I bet she'll teach the others to jump over the corkline."

"I'm sure she will."

In the late afternoon, the sudden darkening of the sky to the west announced the arrival of a storm front. Huge clouds rolled swiftly toward the *Sarah*, billowing upward thousands of feet, as if seeking to mate with the heavens. The thunderheads, black and boiling at their crowns, hid the sun. Billy stared apprehensively at the line of cumulonimbus sweeping toward them and called to Sarah, "I've never seen anything like those clouds. Better close all the hatches and secure everything that might wash away or get thrown to the deck."

She gave him a worried look and hurried into the cabin.

The wind picked up late in the night and blew near gale force. He took down the mainsail and rigged a small storm jib. Except for the faint compass light, they were surrounded by blackness and the roar of wind and spray. He had never experienced such a powerful open-ocean storm and was awed by its ferocity. Billy gripped the tiller and glanced over his shoulder at the giant dim swells. He knew the danger of being swamped was very real. If a wave broke over their stern, the engulfing torrent could doom the small sloop. Steering by instinct and momentary bursts of brightness when the wind created whitecaps, he fought the heavy swells through the long night as they rolled and pitched their way eastward. The continuous shriek of the storm, and the never-ending pounding of the hull, enveloped them so totally they became one with their wet, violent world. Then came the mother of all swells and it raced for their stern, climbing higher and higher. He saw a lip of whiteness race across its crest. The swell was breaking, and Billy screamed at Sarah to hang on.

He gripped the tiller with all his strength and hoped to God they could escape the mountain of falling water. The great wave suddenly spilled and fell. The hideous, snarling crest shattered itself on the sloop's stern, smashing them and flooding the cockpit. Battering water flowed around them like a flood tide. Water shot up the cabin bulkhead and shorted out the compass light. Water by the ton stopped them dead, and the boat settled into the trough, paralyzed by the overpowering weight of the sea. They had to keep moving or die. Billy reached for the engine switch. As he held his breath, the Atomic Four turned over and over. At last it started and throbbed with life. As the Westsail powered up the backside of a swell, water began draining out of the scuppers, and she floated higher.

Sarah screamed at him, "That was close, wasn't it?"

Billy forced a grin and yelled in return, "Hey, she's a tough lady! Named her after you, right?"

By dawn the sea calmed somewhat, though the huge rolling waves continued rising ominously behind them. With light to judge their size and direction, Billy raised the mainsail. Their increased speed enabled him to surf the Westsail down the steep faces of the tumultuous swells. Sarah shoved the tiller at exactly the right moment, sending the sloop racing along the rolling watery mountains faster than a thirty-two-foot sailboat had any right to go. He yelled at her excitedly, "We gotta be doing fifteen knots! A few days of this, and we'll beat *Salvador* to Costa Rica!"

"We're not racing Benny."

"Hey, I'm a surfer. Just watch!"

He gently pulled the tiller and picked his angle. The bow dipped, and the sloop began charging down and across the face of a swell.

"Can you keep this up till it calms?" Sarah shouted over the rush of water and pummeling wind.

"Hell, yes! Best surfing I've ever had!"

By midafternoon, Billy's arms gave out. He surrendered the helm to Sarah and began coaching her how to surf the boat. She had been watching him for hours and quickly picked up the technique of angling the boat across the steep face of an unbroken swell, racing for the trough, and then cutting back to catch the next swell for another wet and wild ride. Her confidence grew with each successful slide, and Billy's praise sounded sweet in her ears.

At dusk the swells abated and Billy napped beside Sarah as they raced on into the night. When darkness came, Sarah heated canned soup and they shared warm cups of beef-barley broth salted by the spray blowing over the stern. She had never experienced such closeness with anyone and thought, Is it because of the danger we're facing, and putting myself in the hands of someone I totally trust? Could I be falling in love with Billy?

At dawn the seas calmed and the easterly wind held strong and steady throughout the day. Billy took a GPS reading and announced happily, "We've run almost three hundred miles in the last twenty-four hours! Under sail, that's hauling. We'll be off Costa Rica in three days!"

Impulsively, she kissed his ear. Billy laughed and said, "You take it for a while. I'm going to monitor the radio. We may be close enough to the coast to pick up some local fishermen or a commercial station. Hey, maybe we'll get a Sea Fresh Tuna commercial in Spanish!"

He turned the helm over to Sarah and began to sing: "*Sea Fresh Tuna hits the spot. A lotta food value in a can you got. . . .*"

In the cabin, Billy switched on the radio and cycled through the bands, not expecting to receive much except fishing boats and Spanish-language broadcasts. As he turned the frequency selector, a very faint voice, badly garbled and broken with static, came out of the speaker. He had heard the man's Midwestern American accent before. With a shock of recognition, Billy cranked up the volume, grabbed a pencil, and realized it was Arnold transmitting to *Lucky Dragon*. "*Dragon . . . Dragon . . . Dragon . . .* birds and dolphins . . . two-two miles east of your bow . . . Call it eight-four, thirty-five west . . . eight degrees . . . eleven minutes south . . . Get hauling, Santos!"

As Billy scribbled the helicopter's position on the border of a chart, his mind flashed a cascade of mental pictures of flying with Arnold, sighting *Salvador* and Sarah standing with Benny, and swooping over a school of terrified dolphins.

Static ended the pilot's transmission. Billy muttered, "Damn! But I got his position."

He peered at the chart and thought of Chatter. Had she joined the pod Arnold sighted? He felt a sense of foreboding

157

and thought, It's gonna happen again!

He stuck his head outside the cabin and yelled, "Sarah, I found 'em!"

She joined him by the radio. As Billy plotted *Lucky Dragon*'s location on a large scale chart of the eastern tropical Pacific he said, "That was Arnold's voice. I told you about him. Remember? The helicopter pilot."

A minute later he had the tuna clipper's position marked on the chart and turned to Sarah. "The GPS says we're about here. So Gandara should be somewhere over the horizon, maybe thirty-five miles southeast of us. Wow, did we luck out!"

Billy switched the frequency selector, pressed the microphone's transmit switch, and began calling *Salvador*. "Big Ben . . . Big Ben . . . *Sarah* . . . *Sarah* . . . *Sarah* . . . Big Ben . . . Big Ben . . . We've made a radio intercept. Acknowledged . . ."

He broadcast their coded call signs again and again.

There was no returning voice from the ship. "He's too far off. After dark, when reception's better, we'll make contact."

"Now what?"

"Chatter's out there . . . maybe with that pod Arnold spotted. We're going after them, and without Benny if we have to."

Shortly before sunset the wind eased. With the diminishing breeze, the sea calmed and they cruised serenely eastward for the coast. The mast had stopped whipping back and forth and Billy chanced climbing to the crosstree. Sarah watched him holding binoculars and searching the far horizon for *Lucky Dragon*.

She was troubled. Since they had intercepted Arnold's transmission Billy's energy level had exploded. He turned hyper and talked incessantly. All afternoon he had divided his attention between the radar, the radio, and scanning the sea. And with each hour they narrowed the distance between the sloop and tuna clipper. The radio now picked up increasingly frequent transmissions between the ship and helicopter. He had Sarah search the 136–174 MHz band and adjust the squelch control to clear the static. She found that the ship was using the 161.36 marine band and kept the radio tuned to that frequency. Over the exterior speaker came the pilot's voice, and Sarah cranked up the volume so Billy could hear up on the mast. "*Dragon . . . Dragon . . . Dragon . . .* Another pod. Tuna below 'em for sure. . . . Eleven miles west of your bow. . . ."

"Stay on them until we get there," came a voice that Sarah now recognized as *Lucky Dragon*'s captain.

Billy yelled down from the mast. "They'll be turning toward us! Check the radar!"

She glanced at the screen. "There's a faint blip on the fifteen-mile ring."

"Gotta be them!"

He came down from the mast looking worried. "Now, before you start asking questions, here's what I think. Not know. Just think."

He scrunched up his face and explained, "Because it's going to take *Lucky Dragon* at least two hours to reach and corral that pod, they're going to have to make a night set. Since we're heading toward each other, we should be close by the time the net goes out."

She couldn't help herself and asked, "Won't they see us on their radar?"

"Maybe, but we're not a very big return. The radar watch probably thinks we're some small-fry sailboat poking along, which we are. So he isn't gonna be much concerned."

"Then what?"

"If it's dark enough we sail in and cut the net."

She started to speak, but he stopped her. "Don't you understand? Chatter could be in there."

"If they catch us . . . that man . . . he'd kill us both."

"It's her life too."

"Billy, maybe we can cut the net and get them out, but if they see us, there goes the whole operation. For once, look at the big picture. She's only one dolphin. . . ."

"She saved my life."

Not wanting logic, he turned away from her. With a sudden awareness of what was really troubling her, Sarah said cautiously, "You're in love with that dolphin, aren't you?"

For a long moment Billy tried to find the words to answer her. Then he laughed uproariously and said happily, "Hell yes, I love Chatter, but I'm in love with you! There is a big difference, don't you know?"

He reached out for her, and she came into his arms.

Then that voice came from the radio and she felt him tense. *"Atún! . . . Atún! . . . Atún!"*

CHAPTER FIFTEEN

Fifty minutes later they saw a glow of light off their bow. By now, Billy's apprehension was so great he unconsciously whispered, "They're making a set!"

The little Atomic Four's starter motor whined, the engine caught, throbbed softly, and they motored slowly for the clipper. Sarah asked, "Won't they hear us?"

"No chance. It's a madhouse on deck, and the crew's totally concentrating on hauling the net. I hope we get there in time."

Fifteen minutes later they saw the outline of the clipper illuminated by her glaring work lights. Billy dropped sail, explaining that the white cloth would reflect the ship's lights. As they idled on he whispered, "The far side of the net's in darkness. We can ease right up to the corkline and cut it where they won't see us. We'll have to work fast 'cause they'll be hauling in soon."

He grabbed swim fins and a mask, and placed a heavy-duty bolt cutter on the engine cover. She watched him strap a diver's knife to his ankle and asked, "When you cut the net, won't they notice it?"

"How should I know?" he snapped impatiently. "I mean, I don't do this kind of stuff for a living. Ease up, will you?"

As Billy took repeated slow breaths to calm himself, they watched the net coming aboard. He also noticed that Rocha was standing in the seine skiff that was bobbing alongside the ship. Then the Westsail scraped against the corkline, and Billy killed the engine. Inside the net the sea boiled as the entrapped dolphins and frantic tuna surged about. Billy peered into the net, hoping that Chatter would sense him and leap over the rim to freedom. He knew he was dreaming and grabbed the bolt cutters. It took all his strength to sever the corkline. At last the wire strands parted and he fought to draw the net apart, but the opening wouldn't expand.

Billy saw the problem. The nylon webbing would also have to be cut before the opening would be wide enough for the dolphins to escape. He glanced at the clipper. The net was being drawn slowly over the stern, and all was as before.

He pulled on fins and mask, slid silently into the water, and began hacking apart the stands of nylon webbing. Then he swam down the curtain of net, slashing at the strong mesh. Slowly, the gap widened and the first of the dolphins found their way through the opening. Inwardly he screamed at them, That's the way! Go for it, you guys!

As the breach grew wider, more and more dolphins and tuna raced through the opening. Billy turned from the net and kicked for the surface. Suddenly, he was brought to an abrupt halt. He was caught in the slack web. In the darkness ten feet down, he tugged at a tangle of net that had snared the empty sheath of his diver's knife. Go slow, he warned himself. Don't make it any worse.

He knew he had only seconds. Already his need for air was so great that Billy clamped his jaw shut to stop the over-powering desire to open his mouth. To swallow was death. He was a waterman and knew the sensation. Real watermen never drown. They hold their breath, fighting for life, until the oxygen level in their blood drops so low they pass out from anoxia. Lifeguards call it "dry drowning."

His fingers found the straps that held the knife sheath to his ankle and he began peeling back the Velcro fasteners. The upper strap came free. He reached for the lower one, but the mesh was tangled around the clasp. Billy slid the knife blade under the snarl and began sawing at the netting.

In the sloop, Sarah was counting the seconds since Billy had plunged down the face of the net. "Seventy-five . . . seventy-six . . . seventy-seven . . . Oh, God! He's in trouble!"

Sarah grabbed her mask, the emergency deck knife, and a waterproof cockpit flashlight. She dropped over the side, thrust the lens under the surface, and snapped on the beam.

Billy felt some of the strands part, and he shoved the blade under another tangle. His growing panic, his dread of death's nearness, seemed to ease. His mind slipped back to memories of skin-diving for abalone off Southern California.

His greatest fear was to become trapped in an abandoned, free-drifting "ghost net." From that thought his mental focus shifted to the little starbursts of silver light that were beginning to absorb his total attention. What were they? Not constellations. Maybe little glowing jellyfish. He tried to count them. Like stars, he thought. His knife fell from his grasp and he reached out for a pinpoint of light. There was one brighter than all the rest. Before Billy passed out he thought, Yeah, that's the one I want. I'll give it to Sarah.

The bright star was the beam of Sarah's waterproof flashlight. In the dim glow she saw Billy relax and drift downward. She grabbed his hair and stopped his descent. In the faint light, Sarah saw where the net held him and hacked the last strands from his ankle. Driven by fear and love, she towed Billy toward the surface. They rejoined the night beside the boat. She squeezed him around the chest, tilted his head back, and blew into his mouth. After three cycles, Billy gasped, sucked in air, and opened his eyes. He started to cough, but her fingers on his lips stilled the reflex. He nodded that he was okay and weakly climbed the boarding ladder.

On *Lucky Dragon*'s bridge, Captain Gandara peered at the net. He saw that the usually taut corkline had gone slack and parted somewhere beyond the lights. His catch was escaping. That had never happened before, even in the worst of weather. He picked up the bridge walkie-talkie. "Bridge to skiff."

"Right here, captain," came Rocha's instant reply.

"The corkline's broken somewhere along the far end. Run the skiff out there and fix it. Pronto! Pronto!"

Gandara stepped into the bridge and brought out a powerful handheld searchlight, which he plugged into an exterior electric socket. The intense, narrow beam cut through the night

164

and the captain slowly scanned the outer rim of the net.

In the skiff, Rocha turned to grab the throttle. The engine roared, then stalled. It did that sometimes, Rocha knew, when it was hot. He tried again. It caught, sputtered, and died. On the third attempt, the engine started and Rocha idled off following the corkline.

The sound of the skiff's engine booming across the water sent a stab of dread into Billy's guts. He guessed it was Rocha on his way to inspect the corkline. Billy shook off his numbness and decided it was time to escape while they could. He started the engine and eased away from the net. Then came the sudden, intense beam of a searchlight probing along the net. Billy muttered, "They'll see us any second!"

The searchlight flowed over the gray skiff. Billy recognized Rocha standing behind the wheel and peering into the night. He knew they could never outrun the powerful boat. As the sound of the skiff's throbbing engine grew fearfully louder, Sarah dashed into the cabin. Seconds later she stood by Billy, shoving cartridges into the magazine of the Winchester. He lifted a hand to stop her and said, "They'll hear—"

She worked the lever, aimed at the bridge of the clipper and said, "It won't matter if I can—"

The rifle exploded with a roar that carried across the still water. She levered and fired twice more in as many seconds. An instant later the searchlight's beam went out. Though Sarah didn't know it, the .30 caliber bullets missed the light, passed by Gandara's head, and clanged one-two-three into the steel side of the bridge. The captain had been shot at many times. When Gandara heard the impact of the bullets he dropped the searchlight and threw himself on deck. The light's high-intensity bulb shattered. He lay on the deck cursing, wondering who was out there in the darkness, and how had they found him. After a few seconds he cautiously eased to his feet, groped for the searchlight, and found it was smashed.

Beyond the far end of the net, the sloop vanished into the night.

It was fifteen minutes before Billy dared speak. He made a final check of the radar screen, and saw that *Lucky Dragon* had yet to get under way.

"Wow! I didn't know you could shoot a rifle!"

"There are a lot of things we don't know about each other, Billy."

Billy put the boat on autopilot, and they sat close, looking up at the stars. As their tension eased they talked long into the night, about themselves and their dreams and fears, until he fell asleep in her arms. She held him, feeling his heart beat against hers, and thought about how Billy had revealed his basic loneliness and his need to be always on the move to escape responsibility. Sarah had opened up to him and unburdened herself. The realization that she was ambitious and wanted to dominate came as a surprise. He had guessed that her dependence on her father, and being subordinate to him, drove Sarah to excel and want to take control. As they fought to stay awake Billy murmured, "You just need someone you can depend on to love. And it wouldn't be honest if I said I'm that long-term guy. So let's accept that we're here together, and for now let it go at that."

"But what about tomorrow?"

"We radio Benny and pray he finds us before Gandara does."

At dawn Billy gulped a cup of coffee, hung binoculars over his neck, and climbed the mast. *Lucky Dragon* had faded from their radar screen two hours before, but he still felt uneasy. Sarah suspected he was really searching for the dolphin.

She watched Billy staring into the distance and wondered what was going on inside him. Was his attachment to Chatter because the dolphin was some sort of embodiment of all Billy regarded as good and pure, or could it be that he had truly bonded with the animal? She knew that dolphins, and especially Chatter, were beings with such remarkably benevolent behavior that humans would do well to adopt them as role models. She realized she was thinking academically and reflected, Why not be like Billy . . . out there, feelings exposed, going with his gut reaction?

He stood on the crosstree so alert, so animal-like, that Sarah wanted to cry for her love for him. Then she saw him tense and raise the binoculars to the sky. After half a minute he gestured to the east. Sarah heard the distant whomp-whomping of a helicopter. There was only one place it could have come from.

"It's Arnold. He's coming right for us." His warning sent her dashing into the cabin. She grabbed the rifle and rushed out on deck to search the sky.

He dropped down the mast yelling, "Put that damn gun away. And stay in the cabin. It's better if he thinks I'm alone."

The helicopter dove for the sea and skimmed across the surface, headed directly for the sloop. A moment later Arnold was hovering off the bow looking down at Billy. His face betrayed the shock of recognition. He raised a handheld marine radio for Billy to see. Billy reached into the cabin, grabbed the boat's walkie-talkie, and turned it on. "Glad you made it, Billy."

He pressed the transmit button, "So am I, Arnold."

"Was it you who cut the net?"

"What do you think?"

"You cost Gandara a megabuck haul last night. Don't do it again or I'll find you next time."

"Thanks, Arnold. I owe you a big one."

The pilot gave him a wave and began climbing. At a hundred feet he banked the chopper and flew off to the east.

When the rotor's beat subsided, Sarah came out of the cabin and saw Billy turn the sloop on the same heading as the departing helicopter. She asked, "Don't you think we should turn back?"

"Not until I know Chatter's safe."

Billy climbed the mast and began scanning the horizon.

Two hours later thirst and hunger drove Billy from the mast. He drank a pint of water, wolfed down crackers and canned peaches. At the offer of coffee, he relaxed and sat down to ease his cramped muscles. Sarah faced him, saw the fatigue that etched his face, and said, "It's a big ocean, Billy."

"I know it's virtually impossible that I'll find Chatter. But think of it this way . . . maybe she'll find me."

He set his mug on the engine cover and reached out to put his arms around Sarah. "Besides, shooting out that searchlight, you saved my life last night. And I haven't thanked you. So

I thank you now. Nobody could have done better."

"Last night we were very lucky. We can't keep blundering after him. We have to work with Benny."

"Okay. I agree. We'll head straight for Costa Rica, put in at Puntarenas, and join up with *Salvador*. But if you don't mind, I'll keep an eye out for Chatter."

He put the boat on a heading for the coast. Sarah took the helm and he went up the mast again.

Near day's end the wind stopped and Billy joined her in the cockpit. It was still hot and she asked, "How about a swim to cool off?"

He studied the horizon, looking for wind upon the water. The sea was still and he decided it was safe to leave the boat. He threw over a buoy attached to a lifeline and said, "We're so close now, it wouldn't do to have the boat sail away without us."

He plunged over the side and dived deep, kicking downward into the blue-gray zone where colors fade and light rays bend as they pass through a thermocline.

Here was peace. He continued downward until his ears pained and the pressure compressed the air in his lungs. Billy thought, If only I could open my mouth and breathe the sea. Hey, I could be the first water breather. Instant reverse evolution. Could I do it?

He looked up to the surface and saw Sarah watching him far above. He began to stroke toward the sunlight. Near the surface he heard a sudden burst of high-pitched clicks and pings. He spun and looked wildly about. There she was, racing for him. He burst into the air and screamed joyfully, "Chatter!"

The dolphin leaped out of the water, spun, and landed

next to Billy. He reached out for her and she nuzzled her beak against his cheek. There were more echolocating sounds. Suddenly a small pod of dolphins arrived to surround him. Sarah kicked for the boarding ladder and hung on watching Billy as several large males, all clicking and pinging, circled him.

Billy stilled his fear and reached out to touch them. Their sounds grew softer and the dolphins began to brush against him. The energy of their nearness and quivering life force flowed into Billy. At that moment he felt a deep oneness with them, as if he were part of the pod.

"What do they want?" she asked softly.

"I have this strange feeling that they want me to help people understand them."

Her eyes narrowed with disbelief. Billy could only shrug and say defensively, "That's what I think they're telling me."

Then his eyes caught movement behind Sarah. A sudden wind had filled the sail and the boat was moving and he yelled to her. "Get aboard!"

As the sloop sailed away, Billy sprinted for the boarding ladder. He saw Sarah scramble on deck and race to start the engine. The wind grew stronger, and Billy feared he might not make it aboard. Then he saw the ring buoy moving past and grabbed it. Hand over hand, he pulled himself back to the ladder and vaulted over the railing. Sarah had the engine started and had the tiller hard over to come about and pick him up. He gave her a quick grin of thanks and said, "That was close. From now on, no more swimming unless one of us is aboard. And you did great!"

The breeze grew stronger, chilling them as the water evaporated from their bodies. They pulled on sweatshirts and watched Chatter take up her customary position off the bow. The pod accompanied them for a few minutes and then veered away. To Billy's relief, Chatter remained.

Later, when the strangeness of the encounter subsided, he told Sarah of the feelings he'd had underwater.

"The sun's getting to you, Billy, or you're losing it. In all the research on dolphins, and in all the recorded human-dolphin contact, no one has truly been able to communicate with them. You're a great guy, but . . ."

"I don't give a damn about all those studies and research, I just know what happened between them and me."

CHAPTER SIXTEEN

Three days later their voyage from Fiji to Central America ended with Sarah's excited cry, "Billy! There's land!"

She stood on the cabin top and gestured eastward. He joined her. In the distance they saw a hazy, far-off landmass rising out of the horizon capped with billowing altocumulus clouds. He put an arm around her and with evident relief said, "We did it, babe. We crossed most of the Pacific Ocean in a pea pod of a thirty-two-foot sloop."

"And saved a lot of dolphins along the way,"

"Puntarenas, here we come, and about time. We're almost out of water."

He kissed her lightly and added, "Wouldn't it be nice to take a long hot bath, and sleep in a bed more than two feet wide that doesn't rock?"

"And eat oranges and a green salad. Then how about an ice-cream cone?"

Sarah glanced down at Chatter and said, "What about her?"

"She'll do what she has to. Let's play humans for a few days in port."

"And then . . . ?" she asked anxiously.

"We find Benny and go after Gandara!"

Instead of sailing into Puntarenas harbor like a proper yachtsman, Billy dropped the main, started the engine, and powered down the channel. He glanced at Chatter. She had fallen behind and refused to follow them. Billy remarked, "The harbor's probably polluted. She knows where it isn't healthy."

"Aren't you worried about her?"

"She'll be fine. And besides, she wouldn't fit in a bathtub."

She stood on her tiptoes and kissed his ear.

Inside the channel, the harbor widened, and Billy saw that Puntarenas was a major port capable of accepting oceangoing vessels. He told Sarah, "That means there has to be a couple of good restaurants and a hotel. Am I ever hungry for a steak, and a green salad with tomatoes and avocado."

"And how about a cold glass of fresh milk?"

Their food fantasy ended abruptly. Two hundred yards down the harbor channel they saw a black-hulled tuna clipper moored beside some sort of rusted corrugated-steel factory building. Billy grabbed binoculars and focused on *Lucky Dragon*. Through the lenses he saw a tall bearded figure on the bridge leaning over the rail watching tuna being offloaded onto cannery trucks. Billy's gaze shifted to the top of the wheelhouse. The helicopter was missing and he worried. *I hope Arnold didn't crash.*

He grabbed Sarah's arm, pointed to the clipper, and whispered, "How about that. Six thousand miles across the ocean and we end up in the same place. After this, I have to believe in fate."

He passed her the field glasses and she focused on the truck that was waiting for its load of yellowfin. She read a faded sign on its door aloud, "Pescadores Universal. It wasn't fate that brought *Lucky Dragon* here, Billy. That's a Universal Brands cannery."

Billy began singing the jingle, "*Sea Fresh Tuna hits the spot, a lot of nutrition in a can we got. . . .*"

She jabbed an elbow into his side and hissed, "That's not funny, Billy. Now what?"

In answer, he sent the sloop across the channel to the far side of the harbor. When they had docked among a fleet of small commercial fishing boats, Billy said, "After we report to the harbormaster and customs, we're going to find the best hotel in Puntarenas."

"I like your style, Billy goat."

They stepped off the *Sarah* carrying day packs and the video camera case. The sensation of standing on land again brought momentary dizziness, and they held the dock railing waiting for their equilibrium to return. As their legs grew accustomed to solid ground, they walked into town.

Billy pointed to the tastefully lettered sign encased in wrought-iron grillwork over the entrance to a small, well kept two-story hotel, La Casa California, and said, "This place has got to have a bath. Maybe even a hot tub!"

Bougainvillea grew in tangled, colorful profusion around

the stone-walled inner patio. A small fountain in the center of a pool spouted water from the mouth of a bronze tuna. They walked on toward the desk, passing a Coca-Cola machine and an ice maker. Sarah remarked, "Just like a Ramada Inn back home."

There was a tub, hot water, clean white towels, and a wide window that looked out over the red-tiled rooftops of Puntarenas. Sarah inspected the large room, liking the Spanish Colonial furnishing and the little vase of flowers sitting on a chest of drawers. She remarked, "It's five times larger than the cabin. I love it." She put her arms around Billy and said with utmost sincerity, "Thank you for getting us here alive. Now for a bath, and afterward I'm going to get my hair done."

Billy climbed out of the tub and thought about cutting off his beard. He glanced at his reflection in the steamy mirror and saw a different person. He looked older, harder, with sun-squint wrinkles about his eyes. Then he remembered why he had grown the beard and said, "While you're being styled, I'm going back to the harbor and shoot some video of *Lucky Dragon* unloading."

"Please be careful."

"Not to worry. We'll meet back here at sundown. Then take a walk along the harbor and have dinner."

She smiled brightly. Billy saw a glint of anticipation in her eyes and thought, I guess it's true. Women like to be romanced.

A hundred and fifty feet from *Lucky Dragon*'s long dark hull, Billy hid behind stacks of cardboard cartons and triggered the camera. He was close enough to hear Santos shouting orders to the stevedores and the metallic clank of deck winches hoisting out clusters of frozen yellowfin. He panned from the unloading to the clipper's bridge. Through the viewfinder he saw Captain Gandara talking with a Latino cannery representative who leaned against the railing that Billy had so painstakingly varnished only weeks before.

Billy panned slowly downward, following a cluster of tuna being loaded onto a truck. Then he heard the sound of a helicopter approaching. To the west he saw the blue-gray copter descending toward the ship. A minute later Arnold settled the Hughes gently on the landing pad. Billy had to admire the man's skill and gave a silent thanks that he was still among the flying. He taped the pilot as he jumped out of the cockpit and dropped down the ladder without stepping onto a rung. Arnold hurried to the bridge and joined Gandara. The pilot seemed excited, and Billy thought, At least he was sober enough to land.

His felt a moment of panic as he saw a group of *Lucky Dragon*'s crew walking along the dock toward him. He recognized the old seaman from the mess hall who had an appetite for dolphin stew and murmured, "I gotta get out of here."

Billy left the docks to explore the commercial area of Puntarenas. He was hungry and thought, It's time for that steak and salad.

The crowded restaurant was clean and busy. Prosperous businessmen talked softly as if they were making deals and didn't want others to overhear. Billy paused at the entrance and saw there was a small table available at the rear where he could watch the door. He glanced up and down the sidewalk, entered, and seated himself. He placed the camera case between his feet, and the waitress arrived to offer a menu and a smile. He studied the list and thanked Miss Montoya, his high school Spanish teacher, for helping him acquire a rudimentary vocabulary. He recognized *ensalada*, *bistec*, and *papas fritas* and ordered his lunch.

With an overflowing plate before him, Billy shifted his attention from the businessmen to satisfying his cravings. The taste of lettuce, tomatoes, sliced cucumber, fried potatoes, and a not-so-tender steak brought a contented glow. He chewed the last bite of steak, glanced toward the door, and choked. Shoving his way into the restaurant came Gandara, the chief engineer, and the Latino cannery buyer. They moved through the room until the manager intercepted them and seated the three a few tables away. Billy fought down panic, picked up the menu, and held it over his face. He looked for a way to escape. Was there a bathroom with a window leading to a back alley? There might be, but that would mean standing and revealing himself. *Now what do I do?* he thought.

The restaurant was packed, and Billy saw two business types eyeing his table with a look of pained impatience. A moment later the waitress presented his check. He fished out his wallet and left enough on the table to pay his bill. Remembering the camera case, Billy picked it up and walked nonchalantly for the exit. Fearful of being seen, he kept his face turned away from Gandara and the others, and hurried past them.

As a potted flower turns to sunlight, Billy involuntarily glanced at the captain. Their eyes met. Gandara's went wide with surprise. Before he could escape, the captain quickly stood and blocked his way. Gandara's hand shot out and he seized Billy's wrist. Then the captain forced him into a chair. As Billy sat, he placed the camera case by his leg and hoped it was out of sight. With more warmth that Billy expected, Gandara said amiably, "I'm glad you made it, *niño*."

"No thanks to you, captain."

"Who picked you up?"

"I paddled my surfboard back."

Billy saw Gandara's look of admiration and the captain said pleasantly, "You're a strong young man. You would. And I owe you a month's pay. Make it six months . . . if you'll forgive my sailing off so rapidly."

Billy thought fast. He would agree to anything to escape the man's mocking smile. From deep inside came a decision to stand up to him and finish what he started. "It's a deal. I'll take the money, and I want my job back."

Gandara's smile faded and Billy added, "I need the money to get home."

Billy watched him consider. He wondered why he had been so foolish. Was it hate for this man? Before he could think it through, the captain said, "Your time aboard will not be so happy, *niño*."

"I just want to get home."

"Very well. You will be working in the galley, and there will be no more jumping into the net. Collect your gear and report to Mr. Santos before midnight. I'm sure he will greet you warmly."

With a nod, the captain dismissed him. For a moment Billy stared into the older man's aristocratic face. Gandara's expression hardened, and Billy sensed there was murder behind his cold, hard eyes. He picked up the camera case and walked away, forcing himself to stand tall. He stepped outside into the moist heat of the street. After a deep breath to calm himself Billy noticed that the hand gripping the aluminum case ached. He switched it to his other and saw his fingers were trembling. He asked himself, Why didn't Gandara say anything about the case? He thought for a moment and decided: *Because his attention was totally on me . . . like a shark about to jaw down on a fish. Now, what do I tell Sarah?*

CHAPTER SEVENTEEN

He sat in the Westsail's cabin, listening to Benny Seeger's distant voice crackle out of the shortwave radio's speaker. Reception was good, and Billy explained how he had managed to get back aboard *Lucky Dragon*. Benny's calm response helped ease his tension. "We're a day's sail west of Puntarenas. We should make port about three in the afternoon tomorrow. Over."

"He's sailing in the morning, Benny."

"Okay. Take the camera and that handheld marine band radio. Use channel 17. We'll be monitoring you full-time. And Billy, shoot as much tape as you can without endangering yourself. Over."

"I'll tell Sarah you'll pick her up here. She's at the Hotel California. The sloop's at the commercial dock, that's the north side of the harbor."

"Will do. And Billy, he's going to be watching you. Be careful, son."

He liked Seeger's concern, liked being called "son," but it was no time for sentiment, and Billy ended the transmission. "You're talking to an expert. See you, Dad. *Sarah* out."

Billy switched off the radio and turned to open a locker. Inside, crumpled and stiff with dried salt, lay his waterproof getaway pack. He found a plastic bottle, filled it with water, and stuffed it inside the bag and thought, Here we go again. Do I tempt fate and bring my surfboard? Maybe I'd better, to stay in character. And how do I get the camera and radio aboard?

He thought of a way that might work. What's next? he thought. Tell Sarah what happened. That's not going to be easy.

Sarah looked so different that it startled him. Her hair color was the same, but the close-cropped cut, plus the dress and a smear of soft red across her lips, made her look older, sophisticated. He told her of his encounter with Gandara and the radio talk with Benny. When she got over her shock, her eyes flashed anger. "Don't you understand? He's letting you back aboard to kill you. I mean you could go to the law and put him away for attempted murder. They're witnesses to what he did to you. And you're a witness to what he has been doing!"

"Where do I file charges? Cuba? Nigeria? Taiwan?"

He took a deep breath and went on. "Sarah, I have to do this. What's my life worth if I don't?"

She saw the futility of arguing with him. There before her stood a real man, hard, determined, and focused on having his way. She perceived that other men, over the course of humankind, had stood before fearful women and told them the same sort of nonsense before going off to kill each other. And she responded, she was sure, like all those anguished women in the past and said, "Oh, Billy. I love you."

They embraced. Billy pulled away, fighting back tears. He mumbled that everything would work out, and told Sarah not to worry because he would be careful and come back to her. She could only shake her head and let her own tears flow. He wiped them away with a finger, reached for his day pack, and stepped out the door.

He waited in the dark among the cardboard cartons of tuna cans until the dock was deserted. It was only nine o'clock, but that was a good time to make his move. This early, most of the crew would be in town eating and drinking. Later they would return drunk and happy, or fighting mean. This was the time. He fitted the straps of the getaway bag over his shoulders. The waterproof bag was heavy now, weighted with rocks he had picked up along the road to the harbor. Billy made a final check of the dock and moved from among the cartons. He was wearing his surfing trunks and carried swim fins. Tucked into the waistband of his trunks was a coil of fishing line with a large treble hook and a four-ounce lead sinker tied to one end. The hook's sharp points were sunk into bits of wine bottle cork to keep them from snagging his skin. He eased off the dock and dropped into the warm, placid water. The tide was flowing in, and most of the garbage was moving deeper into the harbor. Five minutes later he was floating off *Lucky Dragon*'s stern.

Above him the seine skiff rested on the huge net. He checked for movement, listened for sounds of talking, and sniffed the air for cigarette smoke. Nothing. Billy pulled the coil of line out of his trunks and removed the cork from the hooks. With a final searching glance, he tossed the weighted line. The hooks dropped amid the net and snagged the webbing. He gave the line a tug and it grew taut. He then tied the other end of the line to his waterproof getaway bag and released the pack. The weight of the rocks pulled the bag under and it sank out of sight. Billy thought, You'd better not leak, or there goes a good camera and radio.

When his hair was dry, Billy stood, shouldered his day pack, and picked up the surfboard. With a feeling of dread, he walked along the harbor seawall for *Lucky Dragon*.

As Billy reached the top of the gangplank he saw Santos grinning at him contemptuously. "The captain told me you would be coming aboard. You must really want to get home, *niño*."

Billy put his gear and surfboard down on the deck and said lightly, "I've got a girl. . . ."

"So, the artist is also romantic."

Santos kicked his pack lightly and said, "Everything out, *niño*."

Billy had expected the routine and spread his belongings across the deck. The mate prodded his things with the point of a shoe, seemed satisfied Billy wasn't smuggling contraband aboard, and asked, "Your little bag? The one with the things to survive. Did it save you?"

"It helped."

"Where is it now, *niño*?"

"It sank."

The mate sensed that Billy might be teasing him, or lying, and growled, " You will bunk in Mr. Lessing's cabin. Now, report to the galley, and there you stay, *niño*."

The cook and his helper had left the galley a mess. The wide stainless steel sink was coated with grease, the deck needed sweeping and a mop, the refrigerator held spoiling food, and there was no coffee in the urn for the returning crew. He set to work, and in an hour had the galley in order. As coffee brewed, he slumped into a chair thinking about Sarah and Chatter and what would happen next. His thoughts were snapped back to the mess hall by the sound of Arnold's slurred, alcoholic voice. Billy stood and quickly retreated to the galley.

"All that talk about overfishing," Arnold proclaimed loudly, "is bullshit. Flying today I saw more pods than ever . . . less than a day's sail from port."

They stepped into the mess and saw Billy behind the serving counter. The captain nudged Arnold and pointed at Billy. "There he is, Mr. Lessing. Our prodigal Billy returned from the sea. Certainly by an act of God. Wouldn't you agree, Mr. Lessing?"

The pilot eyed Billy, smiled drunkenly, and said with a shrug, "With Billy, who knows?"

Gandara leaned on the counter and stared at the young man, challenging him with his intense green eyes. "Tell me, *niño* . . . are you a ghost come back to haunt me?"

"I'm real enough, captain. Want a cup of coffee? I just

made a fresh pot. Fix you a ham-and-cheese sandwich if you'd like one."

Without waiting for a reply, Billy set three mugs and cream and sugar on the counter, and took the pot from the stove. He poured, and the captain asked, "Why did you come back, *niño*?"

Billy filled the mugs and thought about an answer.

"Could it be that you seek revenge?" Gandara said, almost whispering.

Billy leaned closer to the captain. "Revenge has nothing to do with it."

"Then why? And I want the truth."

"I think what happened to me, after you sailed away, was that I learned to love life."

The captain considered his words carefully, as if he had just heard a profound statement. Trying to comprehend Billy, he said, "You are a very complex young man, or so simple that it is a miracle you are still alive."

"You take your pick, captain."

Gandara looked beyond Billy and surveyed the galley. "You make good coffee, *niño*. And you've cleaned the galley. Do your work well, honor my ship, and you'll finish the voyage."

He took a mug and started for the deck. Arnold followed him and Billy heard Gandara tell the pilot, "With any luck, Mr. Lessing, you'll find those pods again and we'll be back in a week with full freezers."

Arnold glanced over his shoulder at Billy and gave him a concerned look of warning.

* * *

When the crew had come aboard, and the ship was quiet, Billy left the galley and silently moved for the stern. He reached the dark mound of the net and began climbing over the pile of mesh. Near the seine skiff he began feeling for his fishing line. After a few anxious moments his fingers touched the hook, and he slowly hauled in his getaway bag. As he shook the water from it a nearby sound of someone coughing caused him to freeze.

"So, what did you catch, Billy?" Rocha asked softly as he stood up in the skiff.

Billy decided on honesty. "Stuff I don't want Gandara to see."

"I could tell him."

"I wish you wouldn't."

"You stay out of my skiff, and I'll think about it."

"I'm a galley slave now. How come you're sleeping in the boat?"

"None of your business."

Billy turned to leave, half expecting to be attacked. Rocha spoke again, softer now. "Billy, would you paint a new name on the skiff?"

He sensed that Rocha was in some sort of emotional turmoil, and that he was reaching out to him. "Sure, any name you like. What's going on, buddy?"

"Maybe I'll tell you later. And Billy, you watch out."

"You know something I should know?"

"Yeah. If you have eyes in the back of your head, keep 'em open."

"Thanks, Rocha. We'll do some fancy lettering tomorrow."

Clutching his bag, Billy turned from the boatman and

walked off into the darkness thinking, What does he know that I don't?

After hiding the camera and radio in the dry stores locker, Billy entered the darkness of Arnold's cabin and heard the pilot snoring. He hoped he was drunk enough not to wake and slide his Colt .45 from under the pillow. Billy eased into the top bunk and listened to Arnold's labored, alcoholic breathing.

His shoulders and neck ached from tension. He forced himself to relax by thinking of swimming with Chatter in a sea of such clarity that he could view the bottom miles below. His fantasy of becoming a water breather swept away his worries, and Billy was carried into an underwater dreamworld where he became the first of a new species of aquatic humans. Chatter was at his side, his guide and companion. He was growing flukes and fins, and his forehead was enlarging like a dolphin's.

At dawn, as Billy worked in the galley under the watchful eyes of the hungover cook, *Lucky Dragon* cruised slowly out of Puntarenas.

Across the channel, obscured amid the fleet of fishing boats, the Westsail's engine started with a rasping sputter. While the motor warmed, Sarah focused binoculars on the black-hulled clipper and thought about Billy deserting her. She knew it was foolish to follow him, but she had to try. *No, that's wrong. Trying doesn't get you anything. I've just got to do it. At least I can learn what heading they're taking, and then radio Benny.*

Lucky Dragon turned at a bend in the channel and vanished from Sarah's sight. She slipped the dock lines and shoved the throttle forward. With the engine roaring full power the boat moved into the channel. Outside of the harbor mouth she saw the clipper and took a compass bearing on the ship. It was heading west-southwest, directly out to sea, and quickly outdistancing her. She entered the cabin and switched on the shortwave radio. "Big Ben . . . Big Ben . . ."

Once outside the harbor Sarah read her position on the GPS receiver and then gave Benny her location and the heading of the clipper.

"Okay, Sarah. You did fine. Now I want you to sail on that same heading. We'll intercept you sometime around midday and put the sloop under tow. Over."

"Benny, what can we do?"

"It depends on what Billy does. If they set, and he can give us their coordinates, I can do plenty. The weather looks good, so you shouldn't have any trouble. Get moving, girl. Big Ben out."

She had raised and lowered sails with Billy hundreds of times, had learned to find their location with the GPS computer, and with him at her side, she had surfed the Westsail down huge, rolling swells. Then she remembered they hadn't filled the gas tank, and there were only a few gallons left. She remembered what her father had told her numerous times: *Only a fool runs out of gas.*

She muttered, "Thanks, Dad," shut down the engine, and moved to raise the main. As the sail went up and filled with a steady breeze she thought, So far so good, but can I do it alone?

Behind the stainless-steel serving counter Billy collected soiled dishes from the crew, scraped leftovers into a slop bucket, and racked the crockery inside a massive dishwasher. None of the fisherman looked at him except the old seaman who taunted him with "From what I hear, kid, we'll be making a set before sundown. Then it's dolphin stew. Can't wait. How about you?"

He walked away cackling, and Billy thought, Not if I can help it.

By ten the galley was clean and the cook told him to take a break. On deck, where the breeze cooled him, he leaned on the railing and checked the varnish. "It'll need another coat soon, but for sure I won't be holding the brush."

Watching the sea eased Billy's tension. He stared across the smooth surface searching for any sign of a leaping, spouting dolphin, and thought, Could Chatter know I was aboard? Impossible. And what about her? Is she swimming outside the harbor waiting for me. Or with another pod? I hope she's okay.

He sensed someone approaching and turned to see Arnold. The pilot was carrying his flight gear and a little plastic Igloo beer cooler. He stopped beside Billy and said, "You sure must need a job bad, or something. . . ."

"Call it unfinished business."

"Kid, I gotta warn you. The smallest little slip, and the captain is going to make tuna salad out of you. And you'd better believe it."

"It's my war, Arnold. And you know about war, right?"

The pilot moved closer to Billy so they wouldn't be heard and said, "Yeah, Billy. I know about war. And it drives some men crazy."

Billy didn't feel like listening to any of his philosophical bullshit and snapped, "How long did they lock you up after Afghanistan?"

The pilot's body sagged and his face took on a haunted look. He shook it off, and Billy watched him recover his poise. With a smile of openness Arnold hadn't displayed before, the pilot said, "Long enough, and I'm doing okay. But something's driving you, Billy. And if you don't let it go, you'll join my club."

Billy guessed the pilot was telling him to stay calm for however long he'd be aboard *Lucky Dragon*. When the younger man didn't answer, Arnold put both hands on Billy's shoulders and said, "Whatever you're thinking of doing, keep me out of it, 'cause the edge I'm dancing on is awful damn thin."

"Arnold, did you ever stand up and say no to anything?"

He saw the older man's troubled look return. As the pilot turned away, he said, "Go to hell. . . ."

Billy watched Arnold scale the ladder to the helicopter pad and climb into the Hughes. He thought, Flying off to war again.

The wind had eased, and Sarah began to fear Benny would never find her. She looked down the sloop's wake and then eastward toward the coast. All she could see was a wide, endless expanse of ocean. With a feeling of panic, Sarah realized she had sailed out of sight of land. She calmed herself and thought, I can read a compass, hold a proper course, and work the navigation computer. And I stood hundreds of watches while Billy slept. I'll be fine. I'd better radio Benny and give him another position report.

Sarah engaged the autopilot, checked the horizon for shipping, and ducked into the cabin. She took a GPS reading, and then another. Her latitude and longitude, displayed on the digital readout, differed by only a tiny fraction of a degree. She reasoned that the discrepancy was due to the distance the boat had sailed between readings. She turned on the shortwave, punched in Benny's frequency, and began transmitting, "Big Ben . . . Big Ben . . . Big Ben . . . "

Benny's voice boomed out of the cabin speaker, acknowledging Sarah's message, and she gave her position. His reply eased Sarah's concern. "We have you on radar, so you should see *Salvador* in twenty minutes or so. Watch for us off your port side."

"You're sure?"

"Just pick up the glasses and see for yourself. Big Ben out."

Like Billy had done so many times, she slung the binoculars' strap around her neck and began climbing the slender aluminum mast. She didn't like heights, didn't like clinging to the salt-encrusted, corroding metal that swayed back and forth.

The distance between the mast's tiny footholds was uncomfortably wide, and Sarah struggled upward from rung to rung. Her arm and shoulder strength, she was forced admit, was not as great as Billy's, and she tired quickly. After a stop to rest, she reached the crosstree and stepped out on the spreader bar. Thirty feet above the deck Sarah balanced on the narrow, swaying perch with one arm around the mast. She looked down at the heaving sea and suddenly felt dizzy. The binoculars fell from her other hand to dangle around her neck, and she wrapped both arms around the mast. The swells, coming side on, increased the rocking of the boat and the arc of the mast's sway. She felt nauseated, and panic again gripped her. Sarah clenched the mast tighter until the feeling passed and lifted the binoculars. In the distant haze, approaching from the north, she saw *Salvador*'s faint outline. She waved and cried out, "Come get me, Benny."

She continued to stare at the old minesweeper, watching it slowly take on its distinct, familiar shape. The magnified horizon climbed and fell in her vision and the dizziness returned. Her mind spun and she willed herself to leave the mast, but she couldn't force her hands to release their hold. Clenching her teeth, she told herself, "I have to get down and meet Benny."

She released her grip on the mast and started down. At that moment a large swell hit the boat abeam. The hull rolled, and the mast swayed until it was leaning over the water. She looked down, saw the ocean below, and felt certain the boat was going to tip over. The unexpected lurching caused Sarah's hands to slip. Then she lost her footing and fell. Twisting and turning, she screamed in fear. Her left foot grazed the railing and she slammed into the sea. Barely conscious, Sarah sensed she was underwater and struggled for the surface. Several seconds later her head emerged into sunlight and air. She gasped and looked for the boat. The sloop was only feet away, but it was sailing off without her. She sprinted after the boat that quickly receded beyond her reach. Panting from exhaustion, she watched the sloop sail on. Her eyes held on the little pair of leaping dolphins Billy had painted on each side of her name. At that moment she realized that they looked like Chatter.

CHAPTER EIGHTEEN

Billy sat cross-legged at the stern of the battleship gray seine skiff with lettering spelling WARRIOR on the freshly painted transom. He roughed in the new name with a pencil and turned to face Rocha. The young Latino's face betrayed an inner anguish, and Billy wondered what was eating at his guts. Rather than play psychiatrist, he asked, "Those letters big enough for you?"

"Yeah, they'll do."

He couldn't subdue his curiosity and asked, "How come the new name? I thought Yolanda was great."

"You ask too many questions, bro. What is it with you? You come aboard my home and everything goes crazy."

"Your home?"

"Yeah, from one jungle to another, but this one floats."

"You never told me about Yolanda."

"My business."

He finished outlining the last "R" when the klaxon's jarring blast reverberated throughout the clipper. They froze waiting for the announcement. Then Gandara's voice boomed out of the deck loudspeakers. *"Atún! . . . Atún . . . ! Atún . . . !"*

They looked at each other and Rocha said, "See you later, gotta go to work."

"No! Tell me what happened. Right now. We got time! If you don't, you're never going to let it go! What happened?"

He grabbed Rocha and forced him to sit on the net. With a look of anguish, Rocha slowly began, "Me and Yolanda went out one night. Some guys showed up to hassle my guys. There was a fight. Someone pulled a gun. I pulled mine. He shot. I shot back and Yolanda was in the middle. She died. She was eighteen, my wife . . . The cops came after me. So here I am."

"And you can't go home?

"I'm wanted for murder."

Rocha began crying, then turned and climbed into the skiff. Billy wanted to reach for him, comfort him. Instead, he backed away, not knowing what to say, and feeling disloyal, ran for the galley.

The frantic activity before the net was cast reminded him it was time to get the camera and radio out of hiding. He stopped abruptly by the mast and told himself, Slow down and think this through. Benny's out there somewhere. So first, I have to let him know where I am. And I forgot to bring the GPS. So where am I in latitude and longitude? I haven't a clue. The bridge. Maybe I can find out there. Now how do I pull that off?

* * *

From *Salvador's* bridge, Benny focused binoculars on the sloop. He was expecting Sarah to turn the Westsail toward him. When she didn't, he studied the cockpit and saw that the self-steering was engaged and Sarah wasn't at the helm. Benny grew alarmed, took a bearing off the sloop's wake, and ordered a change in course that sent the minesweeper aft of the sailboat. He thought fearfully, She's either below combing her hair, or she's overboard floating somewhere along the wake.

He keyed the ship's loudspeakers, picked up the mike and yelled, "Everyone on deck right now, and if you've got binoculars, bring 'em!"

With her eyes only inches above the sea, Sarah lost sight of *Salvador*. She had never felt so alone, or so afraid. She was sure that she would never be found, and in the hours left, death would come by drowning. She clung to one hope. Benny would find the sloop, and would begin searching for her. She looked at the sun. How many hours of daylight left—three, four? And sharks? Maybe, but not likely, unless there was food nearby. "I'm food," she said aloud. Instinctively, Sarah spun, looking around, half expecting to see the massive body of a great white rocketing toward her. There was something coming for her, and her heart stopped. Then she saw the familiar dorsal fin cutting through the water. She yelled at the dolphin, and from her soul came a scream of joyful reprieve: "Chatter!"

Sarah reached out for the dolphin, but Chatter veered aside and swam on. A few yards away, the dolphin put her head underwater and pinged on Sarah. The returning signal told Chatter more than the physical density of the human struggling through the water. The dolphin sensed the fear that she was radiating and began swimming slowly toward her. Chatter heard the woman call across the water, "Chatter, please come." The dolphin responded as she had been conditioned to and swam for the human. She stopped beside Sarah and felt a hand grasp her dorsal fin.

In the galley, Billy filled a carafe with coffee, piled slices of pound cake on a plate, and slid them onto a tray. It might work, he thought; sometimes he orders coffee for the bridge when they make a set.

He hurried along the deck and was almost knocked over by the cowboys readying chase boats for launching. As he ran up the bridge steps he saw Santos out on the wing peering through spotting binoculars. Billy tried to slip past the mate, but he shot out a hand and stopped him. "Pour me one. Three sugars."

Billy obeyed, and Santos grunted something that might mean thanks. He hurried on and carried the tray into the wheelhouse. Gandara was standing beside the chart table plotting a course on a map. He sensed Billy approaching, glanced at him, and then called out to the helmsman, "Head off to the southeast. Make it one, six, three."

Arnold's voice sounded from the bridge speaker. "They're about fifteen miles off, moving slow like they're feeding on bait fish, not too far from Refugio Shoals."

Gandara picked up the mike. "Your position, Mr. Lessing."

The pilot transmitted his location, and the captain moved back to the chart and made a dot on the paper. Billy took a step closer to the map and read the coordinates. Gandara looked up and eyed him suspiciously. Billy moved the coffee tray as if asking where did the captain want it. Gandara motioned to the top of the chart locker along the wall. Billy set the tray down and started for the door.

"What do I owe you for this unexpected kindness?" Gandara asked sarcastically.

"Thought you might want coffee," he said innocently.

"Billy, you do not lie well. Now, what the hell is it you want?"

Billy stood frozen, staring at the tall man's demanding eyes, wondering how he should answer. He started to stammer something about the cook sending him. Then Arnold's voice diverted the captain's attention. "The pod's beginning to move into the shallows. Better come quick, or we'll lose 'em!"

Gandara reached for the mike. "With all speed, Mr. Lessing. *Dragon* out."

As the captain moved for the chart table, Billy eased out of the bridge and ran for the galley. With his heart pounding, he dashed into the dry storage locker and yanked out the scuffed getaway bag. Where could he remove the camera without being seen? Arnold's cabin.

Inside the pilot's quarters, Billy opened the bag and pulled out the handheld marine band radio. When was the last time he'd changed the batteries? He couldn't remember. He told himself, "They'll be okay. They'd better be."

He punched in the clipper's ship-to-air frequency and heard Arnold's excited voice. "*Dragon . . . Dragon . . . Dragon . . .* They've slowed to feed. We got a real circus down here. Come and get 'em, captain!"

He switched to *Salvador*'s frequency, stuffed the radio into the waistband of his jeans, pulled his T-shirt over it, and cautiously stepped outside to transmit free from interference. On deck, in the shadow of the superstructure, and away from the chase boat drivers and the crew assembling aft, he turned on the radio and begin transmitting, "Big Ben . . . Big Ben. Position report. Acknowledge."

"We're ready to copy," a distant voice answered. Billy gave the clipper's latitude and longitude, heading, and estimated speed. He added, "And I'd guess they'll make the set in about fifty to sixty minutes." He wanted to ask where Benny was, and if they had picked up Sarah, but feared his message might be overheard, and shut off the radio.

Over *Salvador*'s bridge speaker Benny listened to Billy's message from the clipper and hoped to hell the college student radio operator had taken down his position correctly. He made mental calculations and estimated they were less than twenty miles from *Lucky Dragon*. Now he had to decide. He wanted Gandara. But there was Sarah. He muttered, "Where the hell are you, girl?"

He swept the binoculars across the sea, trying to imagine the track the sloop had been taking. He felt certain she was somewhere back along that line, floating in the water, maybe waving at him right this minute. He thanked God the sea was reasonably calm and there were still several hours of daylight. If the wind picked up, creating whitecaps, they'd never sight her. He wanted a better vantage point and climbed the mast to the lookout platform. High above the deck, he scanned the water.

He knew, from years at sea, that it was better to use normal vision before binoculars. On his third scan, something that could be a head registered in his peripheral vision. Very slowly, so as not to lose sight of the target, he stared at the far-off object that bobbed up and down. With his focus fixed on it, he raised the glasses. *Got her!* Then he saw that she was clinging to a dolphin's dorsal fin. *Kid, this is your lucky day!*

He bellowed a course change to the helmsman, ordered full speed, and allowed himself a moment of self-congratulation. *At least my eyes haven't aged.*

When Sarah was on the bridge and toweling her hair dry, Benny told her about Billy's message from *Lucky Dragon*. "They're right over the horizon. About an hour and twenty minutes away."

She indicated the dolphin, who had taken up a position off the ship's bow, and said, "It's my guess that's where Chatter was going too. Now what?"

"We stay out of their radar coverage and hope that chopper doesn't spot us. If they make a set, I've got 'em."

"Billy's on board," she said anxiously.

"And you've fallen for him."

Feeling self-conscious, she nodded. "If you sink the clipper, you're as much a pirate as Gandara. Have you thought about that?"

Benny put an arm around her and said, "I want you to put dry clothes on and then stand by the radio operator. If Billy checks in, you get every word of his message down correctly. Now keep off my back for a while."

"And what are you going to do?"

"After I talk with the kids, I'll be up in the mast with my eyeballs pressed against a pair of binoculars."

He called his crew to the bridge and began giving rapid orders. Then he told himself to slow down, speak calmly, and project a confidence he didn't feel.

"We'll do this just like we've practiced. When I decide it's a go, close every hatch, port, and through-hull valve. I need everything that might come loose secured when we ram. You, boat crew and camera people, make the Zodiacs ready to launch. We may have to rescue the crew, or ourselves. Anyone not on duty, get busy and haul all the mattresses up to the bridge. Then line the forward bulkheads with them. When we collide, I want some padding between us and the steel. And you filmmakers, make sure your camera batteries are fully charged, and run a few seconds of tape just to make sure. There won't be a reshoot, you know. After that, boys and girls, get something to eat. When I say we're going for it, put on life jackets, and everyone without a job report to the bridge."

He grinned at them and saw a mixture of fear and excitement on their faces. They were putting their lives in his hands. For a moment he questioned his right to put them in such danger. But knowing all twenty-three had eagerly volunteered eased his concern. Benny finished by saying, "If anyone has anything to say, now's the time." No one had a question. He turned, picked up the binoculars, and started climbing the mast.

On *Lucky Dragon*'s bridge, Gandara sighted through the Steiner twenty-power binoculars and watched a distant flock of birds diving into the frenzied bait fish that the spouting, leaping dolphins had corralled. *This one will be easy. But they're too near the shoals. I don't like that.*

He called to the bridge. "Radar . . . ?"

"The scope's clear."

"Depth . . . ?

"Eighty fathoms, with a rocky bottom, and shallowing."

Santos joined him and asked, "The shoals . . . ?

"Not to worry, Santos. This set will go fast."

Looking concerned, Santos moved off for the aft deck.

Billy stood by the starboard railing and hid the getaway bag under a ten-man fiberglass life-raft container. Glancing aft, he saw Santos by the seine skiff holding a walkie-talkie, talking to a group of fishermen. Rocha and his new deckhand stood in the boat waiting for the order to launch. The cowboys were already chasing dolphins, and he could hear the snarl of their outboards forward of the ship. It wouldn't be long. Billy began taking slow, relaxed breaths, forcing himself to stay calm. He tried to focus on the sea, but the roar of chase boat engines intruded. *Benny, you'd better be out there, 'cause I'm laying it all on the line this time.*

The angry sound of the speedboats diminished and the ship's engine abruptly stopped its throbbing. Billy looked aft and saw the seine skiff drop off the stern. He reached for the radio, brought it close to his lips, and pushed the transmit button.

"Big Ben . . . Big Ben . . . Big Ben."

"We read you," came Sarah's voice, sounding so near Billy feared someone would overhear.

"The net's going out right now."

"We're on the way. Maybe forty minutes."

"Gotta go. Love you, and hurry!"

He switched off the radio and stuffed it back into the bag. He decided to remain in the shadow of the bridge superstructure until the crew began hauling in the catch. He glanced out to sea. The skiff had the seine out and was heading back to complete the encirclement. He looked among the milling, fear-crazed dolphins, searching for Chatter. There were so many this time. Was she among them?

From the railing beside the superstructure Billy had an unobstructed view of the skiff completing the set. He checked to see that no one was watching, took the camera out of the bag, and thought, I might as well get it all.

He started taping with the lens wide, then slowly zoomed in on the seine skiff. He held the focus on Rocha, who was busy leaning over the side connecting the end of the net. When the shackle snapped shut, Rocha looked up and into the lens. Billy kept his finger on the trigger, sure that Rocha was staring directly at him. Then he heard the great power block beginning to draw in the net and saw the dolphins ramming their beaks into the mesh. He slowly panned the lens around the circumference of the net. His artist's eye caught the soft colors and the subtle shading of blue. He went to a wide angle, trying to frame the whole scene, and created an overall master shot. He imagined a future painting and wondered if he would ever be good enough to capture the moment on watercolor paper. His thoughts were broken by a familiar sound. From over the sea came the whomp-whomp of the helicopter, and he watched

Arnold buzzing over the water toward the ship. The pilot flew straight for the bridge, rising at the last moment to circle before setting down on the helipad. Billy tilted the camera and ran off a thirty-second shot of the helicopter landing, then zoomed in on Arnold's face. He saw clearly that the pilot was looking directly at the camera—at him. He thought, He's seen me, and he must have spotted *Salvador*. Now what?

His worry about Arnold ended as a dolphin fell from the net and smashed on deck. Billy widened the angle for a shot of the seine being drawn up the stern and through the tall power block. As the net came aboard, the entangled dolphins and tuna either fell out of the mesh, or were freed by the fishermen. Some, ensnared in the webbing, rode the net upward, and were crushed as they passed through the power block's giant pulley. Billy kept taping, and as his anger and frustration grew, he became more and more careless about remaining in hiding. He wanted to paint it all with the camera—every gory detail of their violent death. He was so focused on making his electronic pictures, he failed to see Arnold charging along the deck for him. The pilot put a hand over the lens and forced the camera down. Billy spun, ready to strike out, and saw Arnold staring at him as if he was in mortal danger. He sensed the pilot was more concerned than angry and stopped resisting him. Arnold grabbed Billy's wrist, drew him back behind the life raft container, and urgently whispered, "If Gandara sees that camera, you're in the sea again, or worse."

"Arnold, they're dying by the hundreds!"

"Save your sympathy for our kind."

Billy knocked his hand away from the camera and shouted, "Leave me alone, damn it!"

Billy sensed Arnold was holding something back. Then he realized, "You didn't tell Gandara about *Salvador*. How come?"

Arnold smiled faintly, as if embarrassed at being found out. "Ah, Billy, you ask too many questions."

"I want to know, Arnold. Come on."

Arnold glanced over the side at the dead and dying dolphins and then turned to Billy. "You and your damn do-gooder innocence kind of rubbed off on me, son."

Billy probed for more. "So you took a stand."

Arnold shook his head sadly as if no good would come of it and walked off.

On the bridge, Gandara leaned out over the starboard wing watching the seine being drawn aboard. He sensed the net was nearly full and estimated the catch would come to twenty tons. He was pleased that it was going so smoothly, and the pod had not entered shallow water. His feeling of satisfaction was shattered by a call from the radar watch. "Contact, captain. A large vessel approaching on the port side, twelve miles out. She just popped up on the screen."

"Speed?" demanded Gandara.

"Fifteen knots."

"Give me depth and bottom."

The helmsman glanced at the depth sounder. "Sixty-two fathoms with a rocky bottom and shallowing."

They were slowly drifting into shallower water, and Gandara knew the current had them. With the net out he had to use the engine sparingly. He glanced forward. Two and a half miles ahead the Refugio Shoals showed white water. He looked to the stern and noticed that the sea surface appeared ruffled. A breeze was picking up and blowing toward the shoals. With the force of the wind against the hull, and the current, they were drifting faster than he liked. Well, they'd have the net aboard long before there was any danger of going aground. But what about the approaching ship? He picked up the bridge phone and called the mast lookout. "There's a vessel heading for us, somewhere off to port, twelve miles out. The moment it's in sight, give me a description of her."

He considered sending Mr. Lessing aloft, but by the time he was in the air, the lookout would have a sighting, and he might need the helicopter later. He picked up a walkie-talkie and called Santos.

"We have a vessel approaching off the port side. Bring the net aboard pronto, Mr. Santos, and to hell with the fish."

Gandara glanced toward the port horizon. Someone was coming for them. Who? He suspected an environmentalist group. He had heard rumors in Puntarenas that *Salvador* was steaming for Costa Rica. Gandara frowned and looked seaward again. The bridge phone rang and he jumped for the receiver. The lookout confirmed his suspicions.

"Looks Navy, captain. Gray. Minesweeper type, about a hundred and ten feet long, and coming right for us. I'd guess it's *Salvador*."

Impatiently he demanded, "How far out, man?"

"Maybe ten miles."

Gandara slammed down the receiver, picked up the walkie-talkie, and called Santos.

"It's *Salvador*. If you can't bring the net aboard in the next fifteen minutes, cut it free."

He put the radio down and keyed the klaxon horn. When the warning blare stopped, Gandara announced, "All hands not working aft, report to your emergency stations."

He hurried inside the wheelhouse, grabbed the second mate, and slapped keys to his quarters into the man's hand. "Open the arms locker and issue all the rifles. Pronto, man. Pronto!"

Gandara checked the radar screen. The oncoming vessel was rapidly narrowing the distance between them. He moved to the sonar display. The bottom was shallowing gradually, but still deep enough that the net wouldn't snag for some time. He ran out on the bridge and lifted the walkie-talkie. "Santos, have the chase boats hauled aboard right now!"

He grabbed binoculars and scanned the horizon. The gray vessel was now visible from the bridge. He had seen it before, but always at a distance, while they were successfully outrunning her. There was no mistake. *Salvador* was steaming for him. He yelled at the helmsman that he was going aft and warned the man that he would personally throw him overboard if the ship went aground on the shoals. With a last look at *Salvador*, Gandara ran from the bridge.

As Billy taped the dead and dying dolphins being thrown to the waiting sharks, he failed to see Gandara racing along the superstructure for the stern. The captain noticed the open getaway bag lying by the life-raft container, slowed momentarily to glance at it, and then ran past Billy without giving him any notice.

Billy kept taping and held the lens on Gandara. The camera's microphone picked up the captain's urgent bellow to hurry the net aboard. A big male spinner fell from the net and crashed on the deck beside the captain. He stepped aside to avoid being struck. Then he turned slowly in Billy's direction and saw him holding the camera. For several seconds he looked at the young man and then walked slowly toward him. His face displayed curiosity, as if he didn't believe what he was seeing. His eyes shifted to the getaway bag and he moved past Billy to pick it up. He reached inside and withdrew the handheld marine radio. In a menacing voice that caused Billy's guts to tighten into a knot Gandara said, "You gave them my position. You brought them here. You're one of them. And now you take pictures!"

With a slow, deliberate movement, Gandara drew his knife from its sheath and seized a small dolphin still quivering in the net. He pulled it free and slit the creature's throat. As its blood spurted on his white tennis shoes, he began butchering the living flesh. He sliced a long strip from the dolphin's flank and held it out to Billy. "You want pretty pictures, *niño*? Here, make pictures of this."

The captain thrust the bloody offering at Billy. He shrank back, and Gandara whipped the strip of dolphin flesh across his face. Stung and horrified by the lashing, Billy jumped aside. Gandara put out his hand for the camera. "Give me that, *niño*. Right now, before I make a dead man out of you."

He was dazed from the blow and stood frozen with dread. As Gandara reached out for him, Billy recoiled and came alive. He turned and fled along the deck in the direction of the bow. Santos ran to stop him. As the mate made a grab for Billy, he swung the camera and it smashed into the man's face. He dashed past Santos, retreating for the bow. He glanced over his shoulder, very much aware that the captain and his knife were right behind. He heard Gandara's commanding yell, "Stop him!"

Billy looked up at the bridge and saw an armed seaman rushing down the steps to intercept him. He raced on before the man could reach the deck and found himself trapped against the high, knife-edged bow. There was no place left to retreat. He spun and saw Gandara was only steps away. The knife gripped in the captain's hand was set for a killing thrust, and the madness that clouded his face left no doubt that he would strike. Billy took the only way of escape left him. Clutching the camera to his chest, he vaulted over the bow and plummeted to the sea far below.

CHAPTER NINETEEN

As Billy fell, he tumbled and fought to turn his body upright so he would plunge into the sea feetfirst. In the microsecond before impact he thought, *The camera. I can't lose the camera.*

He hit the water sideways, and his head smashed into the sea. The violent, slapping blow knocked him unconscious, and the momentum gained during the high fall drove him deep underwater. Twenty feet below, his body's positive buoyancy stopped the descent. For a brief moment Billy hovered between life and death. His sight came back first. What he saw was blurred. He wasn't sure where he was or what had happened. His eyes told him that he was not in daylight. Nor was it night. With a sudden, fearful awareness, he realized he was underwater. He told himself, *Real watermen don't drown.* Then he sensed he was still clutching the camera to his chest and the past few minutes of his life came back in a rush of jumbled, fearful memory images. With a stab of awareness Billy realized, He was really going to kill me.

Now fully conscious, he stroked frantically for the surface. He gasped and looked up at the ship. Gandara was leaning over the railing staring down at him. Even at that distance, he could see the captain's green eyes, narrowed and filled with hate, boring into him. Then he turned away, and Billy was left floating under the clipper's bow. With a feeling of utter hopelessness he asked himself, What the hell do I do now?

He did the only thing possible and began swimming away from *Lucky Dragon* as fast as he could. As his mind began to function, Billy prayed that Benny and Sarah were only minutes away. *Salvador* was his salvation. If they didn't come soon he was dead. He looked across the water. The corkline and the seine skiff floated some three hundred yards away. Rocha and another man stood on the engine cover watching him. Would they help or only stare? Would Gandara order them to run over him as he had the dolphin pod leader?

The captain bounded up the stairs for the bridge and yelled into the wheelhouse, "Where is that ship now?"

"Six, seven miles off and still approaching."

Gandara forced himself to remain calm. "Depth . . . ?"

"Fifty-seven fathoms and holding."

With his frustration growing, Gandara grabbed the wheel and yelled into the bridge, "Give me five knots."

The captain's eyes shifted to the water. Off the starboard side he spotted Billy swimming for the net and sent *Lucky Dragon* after him. The engines' massive power spun the twin four-bladed propellers and the ship moved slowly forward. As it gained speed the knife-edged bow began to swing toward Billy. The clipper was responding sluggishly, and Gandara realized that the drag of the huge net was holding the ship back. He picked up the walkie-talkie again and ordered, "Santos, cut the net free immediately!"

The mate acknowledged the order, and Gandara turned to yell at the radar operator, "Target and depth?"

"Five-six miles. Depth, fifty-one fathoms and shallowing."

He cursed, "That kid! I'll have his ass. Now the net's going to snag on the rocks!"

A moment later the handheld radio brought the mate's report, "It's going overboard now, captain."

Gandara thought quickly. There was still a way to save it. He keyed in the skiff's radio channel. "Rocha, hook on to the net and drag it away from the reef."

"There's a man in the water, captain!"

"Do as I ordered, right now, or you'll join him!"

Freed of the net's drag, *Lucky Dragon* began accelerating rapidly. Billy glanced over his shoulder and saw the clipper's tall bow swinging his way. The hundred and fifty yards separation he had gained from swimming was quickly being eaten up, and the corkline was still far ahead. He asked himself if Gandara would send the clipper across the net and chance entangling the propeller. Billy thought not and sprinted for the seine.

Five miles away, on *Salvador's* bridge, Sarah leaned over the port railing watching the dolphin ride the bow wake. Chatter's effortless slide down the never-ending wave of tumbling white water thrilled her. For the few seconds she had been watching the dolphin she forgot that they were racing on a collision course for a ship two and a half times larger and many tons heavier than the old minesweeper. And then there was the ship's crew.

Suddenly, Chatter leaped forward. With a powerful beat of her fluke, she sped ahead. In all the hours Sarah had observed the dolphin, she had never seen her swim so fast. She was racing directly for the tuna clipper, and Sarah knew by the dolphin's frantic response that Billy must be in danger.

At the same moment, Billy realized there was momentary safety behind the line of floats, and Gandara's attention shifted to *Salvador*. The gray minesweeper was much closer now; close enough for him to see a white wake tumbling off its bow. Gandara picked up the walkie-talkie. "Santos, find Mr. Lessing and bring him to the bridge. Tell him he must be airborne immediately. You'll be flying with him. And Santos, arm yourself."

Then he turned to search the water for the kid.

Benny leaned against a sweat-soiled mattress propped against the bridge control wheel. It was awkward reaching around the thick pad to grip the wheel. When they rammed, he hoped the mattresses would absorb some of the shock. Benny glanced about and saw that his young crew were waiting for his decision. They were now a bit shy of four miles from *Lucky Dragon* and he was determined to ram. He picked up the bridge mike and switched on the public address speakers.

"Okay, people. We're going for it in about fifteen minutes, so get yourselves set."

He turned to look at Sarah, saw the apprehension on her face, and reached out to squeeze her shoulder. "I did this once before to that pirate whaler off Spain and nobody got hurt, remember?"

"But you rammed outside a harbor."

"We're committed now, so don't give me a hard time."

He lifted the binoculars and watched the clipper begin to move ahead. He swung the glasses on her stern and saw that the net was drifting free. He called to Sarah. "Gandara's running for it, but it's not going to do him any good. We're too close now!"

Calculating a new intercept point, Benny made a slight course change. He knew the shoals would prevent Gandara from turning tail and outrunning him. He was set up for a perfect ninety-degree beam attack. If nothing went wrong, he had *Lucky Dragon* in a perfect position to slice open her hull. Then he remembered his promise to Billy. "I'll do my best to take out his stern."

The pounding of the tired Cummings diesel pushing *Salvador* to maximum speed, and the slamming of the hull into the chop sent an urgent vibration into the soles of Benny's bare feet, adding to his growing excitement. He was fully charged, a human bomb of emotions set to explode. Benny wanted to scream out a savage, primal cry to lead his kids into combat, but held it back. They wanted him cool—their big daddy who would save them if anything went wrong.

He stared ahead. Something was going wrong for Gandara. The ship had slowed again and was swinging toward the net. He turned to the spotting binoculars and sighted on the clipper to see what the ship had turned toward, or away from. Through the lenses he saw the faint image of someone in the water swimming for the net. He couldn't be sure who it was, but he had an awful feeling who the swimmer might be. Without thinking, he shouted out, "It's Billy!"

Sarah shoved him aside and peered through the glasses. There was no doubt. The blond hair and beard that had tenderly brushed her cheek so often were his. They were close enough now that she was able to tell he was sprinting, and between strokes, looking over his shoulder. She moved the glasses a fraction of an inch to see what he was escaping from. On the bow of the clipper stood the tall dark man they had seen on the clipper's bridge when it was docked at Puntarenas. With a gasp, Sarah realized he was holding a rifle to his shoulder and the barrel was aimed at Billy.

Billy had no doubt that Gandara would fire. As best he could while holding the camera, he made a surface dive and continued swimming underwater until his need for air drove him to the surface. He sucked in a deep breath and dove again. He was beginning to pant from his desperate exertion. He had to stay on the surface longer and longer between dives, offering Gandara a better target. A second before he made his next plunge, bullets splattered the water around him. Then something slammed against his side and he froze with terror, thinking he had been shot. Off to his left he saw the dark graceful bulk of a dolphin. It was Chatter. She shoved against him and he grabbed her dorsal fin. Billy felt her muscular body quiver against him. She began towing him so rapidly he almost lost his grip. She surfaced to blow and inhale, and bullets pocked the water beside them. He took a deep breath and down they went, deeper this time, until his ears pained from the pressure.

Rocha stood on the engine cover staring at Gandara with shocked disbelief. His eyes jumped from Billy and the dolphin to the captain firing the rifle. He tried to figure out what the hell was going on. With the next explosive roar of the automatic weapon he knew that Gandara was trying to kill Billy. Into his mind came the roar of another gun—a handgun he had fired. For a brief moment he saw Yolanda sprawled on the parking lot blacktop, her blood and brains seeping from a massive hole in what had been the left of the side of her skull.

Rocha shook off the horror of what he had done and jumped from the engine cover. He grabbed the skiff's wheel, jammed the throttle full-forward, and sent the skiff racing for Billy. The bewildered deckhand yelled over the pounding engine, "What the hell is this all about?"

"Something you want no part off," Rocha yelled. "Lie down on the deck and stay there, unless you want to get killed!"

"I wanna know what's going on!" he demanded.

Rocha spun and drove his shoulder into the deckhand's chest. He struck with all the hostility and anger that had been building so long within him, and knocked the boatman over the side. He took the wheel and glanced between Billy and the captain, who was slamming a fresh magazine into the rifle.

"Oh, God. No!" Rocha cried out as he saw Billy's hand slip from the dolphin's fin. There was more sadness to his wail than anger. Billy, he could see, was exhausted, and before the dolphin could take him under again Gandara would have the rifle loaded. He had to shield Billy with the skiff, so he turned the boat to send it between his friend and the captain's aim. He screamed at Gandara, trying to divert his attention. "No! Don't!"

Billy heard Rocha's yell and saw the skiff charging for him. He realized that Rocha was attempting to block Gandara's fire with the boat's hull, and a sudden swell of gratitude surged within him. The skiff thundered toward him and he kicked away from its bow. The engine's booming throb stopped and the boat slowed. He gave Rocha a wave of thanks and threw the camera to him. Rocha caught it and waved back. Then came the sharp *brrrupp* of the automatic rifle and wood splinters exploded from the skiff's hull. Billy looked up at Rocha as he took three bullets in the chest. He was slammed back as if struck by a sledgehammer and driven against the wheel. Rocha's wide dark eyes betrayed his disbelieving shock. He made an unintelligible sound, then shook his head as if denying death, and fell across the engine cover. A profound sadness swept over Billy, darkening his heart. He wanted to cry, to kill, to rip apart Rocha's slayer with his hands. But most of all he wanted to give Rocha his life back. He would live the rest of his days knowing that Rocha had died to save his life. He turned away from the skiff and found Chatter. Overcome by Rocha's death, he put his arms around the dolphin and allowed his head to sink against her side.

When the last spent brass cartridge case was ejected onto the deck and the rifle clicked empty, Gandara reloaded. Out of the corner of his eye he saw Santos and the pilot running across the bridge. He noticed that the mate clutched an assault rifle and Lessing was wearing his army Colt .45. He liked the mate's fierce look.

"Mr. Lessing, you will take off and intercept *Salvador*. And you, Santos, you will fire down on the bridge. Do anything necessary to stop her. We only have a few minutes, so hurry."

Arnold looked at the captain with disbelief. He had heard similar orders many times before. Was it in Cambodia, Laos, Afghanistan? *They're breaking through, go get 'em. We're evacuating Quan-Trang. Take the gunship. They're in the open, you can't miss!* He could still see bodies blown apart and flung across the open rice fields in a bloody aerial butchery.

"Hold on a minute!" Arnold shouted. "They're civilians! And this isn't any damn war."

Gandara shoved the rifle muzzle into the pilot's belly. "It's my war, Mr. Lessing, and I intend to win it."

He turned to the mate. "Santos, you are the one man I can always trust and depend upon. See that he does as I say."

"*A sus ordenes*, Louis," the mate responded, daring to use the captain's first name.

"Thank you, old friend."

Gandara watched Santos prod the pilot up the ladder leading to the bridge heliport. I have a chance now, he thought. And I have been lucky for too many years to be defeated by a boy and a dolphin.

He turned to look for Billy. What he saw shook his momentary feeling of confidence. Less than a half mile ahead of the clipper, the Refugio Shoals showed white water.

Gandara ran aft. As he passed the ladder to the helicopter pad, he glanced up and saw Arnold climbing into the cockpit. Santos was freeing the clips that would release the machine, and Gandara called to him, "You must kill a few or they won't stop. Remember that, Santos!"

The mate waved his understanding and Gandara ran on for the stern thinking, Now for the *niño*.

The captain sprinted across the aft deck and saw a chase boat still hanging from its davit. He climbed aboard, placed the rifle carefully on a thwart, and yelled at the second mate, "Lower me at once!"

He pressed the starter and had the outboard motor running before the speedboat hit the water. As the hull slapped into the sea, Gandara glanced at the bridge and saw that the helicopter's rotor blades were beginning to spin.

Salvador raced on for the clipper—an old rusting wooden-hulled minesweeper challenging a solid modern ship—and the tension among the captain and crew mounted as they converged on *Lucky Dragon*.

Benny lifted the glasses and held his focus on the helicopter. He saw an armed man wearing a cartridge bandolier by the skids and another in the pilot's seat. They're going to strafe us, he realized with dread.

Benny yelled at the crew gathered along the bridge railing, "Everybody inside the wheelhouse and stay away from the windows!"

"Benny, what is it?" Sarah asked.

"They're sending up their chopper to shoot the hell out of us!"

"Where's Billy . . . ?"

"Still in the water with his dolphin! Now get under cover or I'll throw you overboard to join him!"

"I'm staying with you."

Benny shrugged, lifted the glasses, and spotted the chase

boat roaring away from the clipper. He immediately recognized the tall black-bearded man who was steering one-handed and holding an assault rifle with the other. There was nothing he could do now . . . unless. . . . Benny reached for the lanyard that activated the ship's horn and pulled the cord.

The loud, piercing sound of *Salvador*'s klaxon reached Billy. Two miles off he saw the gray minesweeper racing for *Lucky Dragon*. She was throwing a wide wake, and his heart soared with the hope he'd live to see day's end after all. Over the far-off blare of the klaxon he heard the high-pitched whine of an outboard and spun. Gandara was charging toward him. Panic came again as he tried to decide what to do. Climb in the seine skiff and attempt to escape? No. The boat was too slow, and he'd be a perfect target. Keep swimming for the net? Maybe. Would Gandara send the speedboat over the corkline and foul the propeller? Probably. *But it might slow him down.*

Billy called for Chatter. The dolphin came alongside and he grabbed her fin. He pointed to the net and urged, "That way, Chatter. Go on!"

She began towing him toward the net, and Billy looked over his shoulder. Beyond the speedboat he saw the helicopter's rotor blades spinning. He watched Santos step back from the copter's skids and move cautiously around the front of the cabin to the passenger door. *Now it's Arnold's turn to come after me.*

Arnold's hand gripping the control stick was trembling more from fear than from the vibration of the engine. In a second he would have maximum takeoff power. In a second, Santos would be climbing into the cabin. Arnold couldn't wait even that long. He twisted the control stick, changing the blade's pitch, and the helicopter leaped off the bridge. He glanced down and saw Santos swing the rifle upward. Then the rotor blade's downwash lashed the mate, knocking him backward. He sprawled on the helipad and dropped the rifle. As Santos came to his feet Arnold turned the helicopter back toward the bridge. He flew directly at Santos. With a look of terror, the mate flung himself aside and leaped to safety. As Arnold thundered by, he saw Santos falling. He hit the railing, then dropped into the water below. Arnold laughed, reached for a can of beer, and thought, That's one for the good guys, but if I ever land on that ship again, it's good-bye Junior Birdman. Now what? He glanced at the fuel gauges. The tanks were full. He had two hours' flying time, enough to reach shore with twenty minutes to spare. He decided to stick around for a few minutes and see how the war ended.

The corkline was still thirty yards away, and Billy knew that the speedboat would be upon them before they reached the net. He looked back, saw Gandara lift the rifle and fire.

The slamming, bouncing boat spoiled Gandara's aim and the bullets went wild. The rifle flew out of his hands and landed in the boat. Then Chatter dove, taking Billy down with her. They stayed underwater until the dolphin surfaced beside the corkline and Billy pulled himself over the rim. He began swimming into the wide enclosure, hoping that this time the net hadn't trapped any sharks. He looked back and saw Gandara racing toward Chatter. She was outside the corkline and right in the boat's path. Billy screamed at the confused dolphin, knowing that the sound of the snarling propeller was jumbling her senses. "Chatter, come on! Jump! Jump the net!"

The dolphin hesitated as if the low-floating corkline was too much for her. Billy sprinted to help her over the net and pleaded, "Chatter, jump!"

He was sure Chatter would be rammed, and grabbed for her. At the last possible second, with the chase boat only yards away, she made a low, effortless leap over the corkline. As he seized her fin he saw Gandara wasn't going to slow for the net. The bow slammed across the corkline and the heavy propeller shaft snagged on the cable, stopping the boat as if it had hit a wall. Gandara was catapulted out of the driver's seat and flung through the air to land in the sea. He hit hard ten feet forward of the bow and Billy thought, I've got to get that rifle.

As Billy sprinted for the boat, Gandara shook off the impact. The distance between them was too great, and Billy knew he couldn't get the weapon in time.

Gandara's hands were already grasping the gunwale when Chatter attacked. Before he could muscle over the side, the dolphin rammed him, driving the captain into the water. He drew his knife and slashed at the dolphin, but she nimbly avoided the thrust and turned aside. Seizing the moment, Gandara scrambled into the boat and grabbed the rifle. Billy looked up and saw the captain aiming the muzzle at him. Then something more compelling than killing Billy diverted Gandara's attention and he looked off. Billy followed the captain's astonished glance and saw *Salvador* speeding for the clipper on a beam attack. He knew there was not a chance in hell that the minesweeper would fail to ram the clipper.

Gandara also saw that his ship was doomed and turned to Billy. "You did this, *niño!*"

As Gandara lifted his rifle, the rattling *whomp-whomp* of the helicopter roared out of the sky. An instant later the diving, blue-gray cabin of the Hughes filled his vision. The chopper skimmed so low over Gandara that he had to dive aside or be decapitated by a landing skid. His abrupt, defensive reflex sent him tumbling over the boat's side. He hit the water violently, dropping the rifle. He looked wildly about and saw Billy not more than five feet away. Gandara lunged at him, and his knife flashed in the late-afternoon sun. The bright reflection of light off the stainless-steel blade warned Billy, and he twisted away from Gandara's explosive thrust. As Billy retreated, the captain slashed and stabbed at him again and again. His enormous exertion, and the weight of his sodden clothes, quickly exhausted the captain. Billy kept backing away, waiting for his chance. He knew the signs of impending drowning from his beach-lifeguarding days. Gandara was already winded. Seconds later his hips dropped, and he began struggling to keep his chin above water.

It happened quickly. His rage changed abruptly to the shocked look of a man facing death. Gandara faltered and turned back toward the boat. After a few ineffectual strokes he began sinking. Still holding the knife, Gandara slid underwater, his hands clawing ineffectually until they disappeared below the surface.

Billy's mind raced. "It would be so easy to turn my back," he thought. "But I'm a lifeguard, a waterman . . . I can't let him go like that."

He dove along the wavering wall of drifting net. Ten feet below, Billy saw the blurred outline of Gandara entangled in the slack nylon webbing. He would drown, like the thousands of dolphins he had slaughtered. Billy reached him and began pulling the mesh away from the drowning man. The captain sensed Billy by his side. He raised his knife, made a final weak thrust, and went limp.

Billy's desperate need for oxygen was so great he came close to unconsciousness. He took Gandara's knife, cut through the final strand that held the captain, and began slowly swimming him for the surface. Billy knew he wasn't going to make it, and decided to let Gandara go. Before he relaxed his grip, Chatter appeared at his side, offering her fin. He took hold of the dolphin, and she began towing the two humans upward. Sunlight streamed down on them, and Billy looked up. The chase boat was there, still caught in the corkline.

They reached the surface, and Billy grabbed the side of the boat. He felt a faint motion from the man he held and looked into Gandara's face. His eyelids quivered, and Billy knew he would survive. He worked him around to the boat's stern. Holding the captain by the hair, he used the outboard's propeller housing as a step and climbed aboard. With a one . . . two . . . three, Billy pulled the man over the transom and let him collapse on the deck.

Arnold made one more pass over Billy and Gandara. He gave the kid a mock salute and turned the helicopter toward the coast, hoping he had the fuel to make it back to land. With a wry smile he muttered, "Billy, if you survive the next few years, you'll be one hell of a man. Good on you, son."

The sound of *Salvador*'s klaxon boomed across the water,

and Billy spun around to look for the ship. She was bearing down on the clipper, only moments away from colliding.

Braced for the impact, Benny steered the minesweeper toward *Lucky Dragon*. After all the years of being denied this battle, he let his frustration erupt in a wild roar that boomed over *Salvador's* pounding engines.

He felt Sarah's hand on his arm. She was gesturing frantically at a speedboat floating by the net. With a start, Benny saw Billy standing above Gandara, waving at them. He felt cheated and muttered, "Wouldn't you know it. The kid got him first."

He looked ahead to the clipper that loomed large and ominous in front of *Salvador's* onrushing bow. The ship was so close now that Benny could see the crew dashing away from the railing in a frantic attempt to escape the point of impact. Like a flash of light illuminating his basic nature, Benny realized he was attacking more than the ship's dark hull. There were men on her deck, and there was his crew, who might bleed and die in the tangle of ripped and crumpled steel. Benny realized his thrust for vengeance was wrong. He spun the wheel and yelled to the bridge, "Full reverse!"

In the chase boat, Billy grabbed Gandara and hauled the captain upright. Their eyes were drawn to the two ships: the larger barely under way, the smaller bounding in for the kill like an aged, starving wolf.

Billy looked down at the beaten man. He thought of Rocha and the bullets that had taken his life. Now Billy wanted justice.

"Stand up!" he ordered. "I want you to see this."

CHAPTER TWENTY

Billy stared at *Salvador*, waiting impatiently for the impending collision. Pumping his fist up and down in a wild gesture of victory, he cheered Benny onward. The gray ship was so close now that he could see Sarah standing beside Benny, half hidden behind a mattress, bracing herself for the impact. Though her full attention was focused forward, he waved at her and felt a surge of anxiety.

Suddenly, the minesweeper began to slow and veer away from *Lucky Dragon*. Billy couldn't believe what was happening, and he felt a sense of outraged disappointment. Why would Benny back off now? He thought he knew. Benny had decided not to chance taking a life. Would Billy have done the same if his hands were on *Salvador*'s wheel? He glanced at Gandara. The captain was staring at *Salvador*, suddenly aware that his ship might survive. He met Billy's unbelieving look with a faint contemptuous smile. Then his hopes faded, and defeat clouded his face.

Billy looked back at the gray minesweeper. Her battering-ram bow wasn't changing heading fast enough, and collision was only seconds away.

Gandara gave a muted moan of anguish. An instant later, *Salvador* drove her prow deep into the clipper's stern. A scream of ripping steel howled across the water followed by the grinding screech of the minesweeper's armored bow climbing up the side of the clipper. Then she sank back, revealing a torn, gaping laceration in *Lucky Dragon*'s side. Water cascaded into the ragged breach, ton after ton of fatal weight.

Billy stared wide-eyed at the devastation, only half-aware that Chatter was rising out of the sea alongside the boat, clicking at him. When he heard the dolphin, he leaned over the side and lovingly stroked her head. She sank back into the water and he glanced at Gandara, who was slumped in defeat, staring at Chatter. The captain shook his head in bewilderment.

Billy had to acknowledge Chatter and leave the captain with a final wound that would never heal. He reached out for the dolphin again and harshly told Gandara, "She's the one who saved me when you sailed off, and if she hadn't, you'd still be killing them."

The captain turned from Billy's accusing stare to watch his ship slowly sinking. As seawater flooded *Lucky Dragon*'s hull, the crew began frantically launching chase boats and life rafts. Billy noticed that Santos was among them, directing the abandonment of the ship. He knew that that meant there was no chance the pumps would keep her afloat. Then he saw the gray seine skiff idling toward them. The shocked boatman held up the video camera and then tossed it to Billy. "What do I do with Rocha?"

"We'll figure it out later. Go help your crew now."

The boatman motored off for the sinking vessel, leaving Billy with Gandara. Billy held back his feelings of sadness and anger. The whole crazy ordeal would soon be over. Then what? He glanced at the Sony. It was ruined, but he suspected that the tape would be usable. He stared at the minesweeper now drifting alongside the clipper. Her bow was crushed and shoved inward some three feet, but the ship seemed to be floating on an even keel. At *Salvador*'s stern the boat crews and camera people were launching the Zodiacs. He saw Sarah climb aboard one and step to the bow. The outboards roared and the high-speed inflatable raced toward him. He felt a glow of warmth and love, and a tremendous release of tension that left him light-headed and wanting to hold her.

The Zodiac raced up, turned broadside to him, and the engine stopped. Billy and Sarah looked at each other. Their smiles drew them together. Billy stepped aboard the inflatable and put his arms around Sarah. He hugged her gently and all the tension and sadness of Rocha's death started his tears flowing. Sarah said softly, "It's over, Billy."

"Not yet. Not until we hand Gandara over to Benny and release the dolphins."

"And then . . . ?"

He gestured for the captain to board the Zodiac, then turned to Sarah.

"There's Rocha. And after that, I just don't know. . . ."

The Zodiac scraped against *Salvador's* boarding ladder, and Billy tied the boat fast. Above them, Benny stared down at Gandara. His face still showed tension, but there was no other expression to reveal his thoughts. The chase was over. Gandara glanced at *Lucky Dragon*. Her stern was underwater now and the crew were aboard life rafts, chase boats, and the net skiff. Benny gave a cold, emotionless order: "Get that man aboard. I want his crew to see who's in command now."

Billy followed Gandara up the steep, slippery ladder. The exhausted captain, shivering from shock and chill, forced himself upward rung by rung. No one reached out to help him onto the deck. Then Gandara was standing face to face with Benny Seeger. Both men were oblivious to the camera crew taping their meeting. Gandara forced himself to stand taller, attempting a show of dignity. "My crew needs assistance. As one captain to another . . ."

"I'll see that they have food and water and get safely to land, but you no longer have a command."

"I protest—"

"Your protest will be recorded in my report, but I tell you this, you murdered in cold blood a young man who was attempting to save one of my crew."

With a glance at Billy, he added, "And there are a number of witnesses. It would be within my rights to put you on trial for murder on the high seas, and if you are convicted, I could legally order you hanged. But you'll hang one way or another. And finally, you'll never kill another dolphin."

Benny turned to stare at the sinking tuna clipper. Gandara followed his gaze.

At that moment *Lucky Dragon*'s stern went fully under. Five minutes later the rest of the hull quickly sank, and the graceful clipper went to her watery grave off the Refugio Shoals.

Seeger ordered Gandara below to be locked in a cabin, then turned to Billy. "There are a few things that need to be done. First cut the net and let the dolphins out. You know how to do that."

He didn't like Seeger giving him orders. "Yeah, Benny, I know how to do that."

"And then bring that young man's body back here."

Billy was bone-weary and wanted to protest he'd done enough today, but he had to say good-bye to Rocha, see that he was buried with respect, and close that chapter of his life. Billy started for the boarding ladder and saw Sarah watching Benny with admiration. The captain put an arm around her shoulder and Billy heard him say, "If that tape Billy shot survived, we've got a fund-raising gold mine. And we'll need footage of that dead kid's body. . . ."

Billy went down the ladder thinking, Right, Benny, business as usual.

Chatter joined Billy as he steered the Zodiac for the drifting net. "That net's going to keep killing if it's not secured. Benny can handle that. Okay, Chatter, let's free your friends."

The dolphin surged ahead, leaped over the corkline, and dove into the net. Surprised by Chatter's unexpected behavior, Billy looked over the rim and saw her swimming amid the trapped dolphins. Then she shot to the surface and easily leaped out of the net. A moment later, several dolphins followed Chatter's example and jumped over the corkline. Within minutes the whole pod had escaped and were racing off. He could only guess that they were following Chatter's example. Or had she taught them? And if she could teach them, could she teach others? Then maybe Chatter could help them learn to stay the hell away from tuna clippers.

He looked for Chatter. She was nowhere in sight. He felt a deep anxiety. *Did she go with them?*

When Rocha's body was aboard *Salvador*, Billy helped place him in the ship's cold storage locker. In the chilly confined refrigerator, he remembered the day the Fijian boatman slid off the stretcher and landed on the Suva dock. He wanted Rocha treated better and insisted he be wrapped in a blanket. As a final gesture of respect, Billy laid a clean galley towel over his face and wished him well on his next voyage.

Billy returned to the deck and leaned on the railing staring at the little sloop he and Sarah had sailed such a long difficult way. She was weather-beaten, but still seaworthy, and there on the cabin roof was his surfboard. It had been a while since he'd caught a wave. Maybe he'd earned a few days of surfing. His musing was interrupted by Sarah's voice: "Billy, we need you."

He turned and saw her leading the camera and sound person toward him. "I know this will be hard for you, but we need your story in detail, for the media, and the court."

Sarah did not push, and she gave Billy time to relax. When he was at ease, she directed him and shaped her questions so he would respond with a complete sentence. Billy soon forgot the camera and just talked, leaving nothing out. He noticed Sarah's discomfort as he described falling in love with her. An hour later, fed up with her probing questions, he waved the camera away. She protested, "Billy, we're not through."

"I am. Too much has happened today. You're scrambling my brain. Come on, Sarah. Get off this TV reporter stuff."

She stiffened and pleaded, "Just a few minutes more."

Benny, who had watched the interview, stepped between Billy and the camera. "It's okay, Sarah. He's beat. We're all beat. We can pick up tomorrow."

"I won't be here tomorrow," Billy said softly.

He glanced at the Westsail and then faced Sarah. "I'll be aboard the sloop. Want to sail with me again?"

She thought a long moment and shook her head. "My life's not about sailing with you. And I don't need a perfect wave or a dolphin for a friend. Benny needs me, and I need to be a part of what he's about. And you've got Chatter."

Billy nodded, reached into a pocket, and turned to Benny. In his open hand Billy held the tiny digital videotape from the Sony camcorder. "It will play, Benny. Not a drop of water inside the case."

Billy juggled the cassette from one hand to another as if he might throw it overboard. Benny caught his meaning. "Tell me what you want, Billy."

Billy took a deep breath, "You owe me big-time."

"I grant you that."

"I want the Westsail, free and clear, with no strings attached."

"She's yours."

Saying anything more would only prolong the pain. He handed Benny the tape, turned to Sarah, and placed his fingertips on her cheeks. She was crying. An overpowering longing to be with her swelled within him. The love was there, but that was not enough. He knew if he stayed he'd become a face-the-cameras media darling to be trotted out at fund-raisers. *Hell with that. I've my own life to follow. And if I can do any good for this world I'll do it my way.*

He studied Sarah's face and murmured, "Have a good life."

Turning impulsively, Billy vaulted over *Salvador*'s railing. He dropped cleanly into the water and began swimming for the Westsail. He was free of them and on his own again. His mind raced ahead. He would follow Chatter, if she came back, and help her teach other dolphins to escape the nets. No. That wasn't enough. He'd do something to help stop fishing tuna swimming with dolphins.

As he swam for the sloop his mind clouded. He asked himself, *Was all this worth Rocha's life? Or anyone's life? I guess I'll never figure that one out.*

He muscled aboard the sloop and ran his hands along the rails of the sleek, graceful surfboard. Where was the last place he had ridden the Becker? Bombora Reef, Fiji. With a faint smile he remembered that last awesome ride. He still felt guilty about his surf taxi and thought, Maybe what happened since then was a wake-up call, a turning point.

Billy untied the towline, freeing himself from *Salvador*, and raised the mainsail. As the sloop slowly eased away from the battered minesweeper, Chatter surfaced beside the cockpit. Billy sensed that his world would find some sort of order now, and he reached to caress the dolphin's head. She quivered under his touch and then leaped forward to take up her usual position off the bow.